In the Quiet

In the Quiet

ADRIENNE ROSS

DELACORTE PRESS

Published by
Delacorte Press
an imprint of
Random House Children's Books
a division of Random House, Inc.
1540 Broadway
New York, New York 10036

Library of Congress Cataloging-in-Publication Data
Ross, Adrienne.
    In the quiet / Adrienne Ross.
        p.   cm.
    Summary: Eleven-year-old Sammy must deal with the death of her
mother and the arrival of her mother's long-lost sister, who has a
special gift.
    ISBN 0-385-32678-5
    [1. Aunts Fiction.   2. Death Fiction.]   I. Title.
PZ7.R71958In   2000
[Fic]—dc21   99-35219
                                                                    CIP

The text of this book is set in 12.5-point Stempel Garamond.
Book design by Debora Smith
Manufactured in the United States of America
March 2000
10   9   8   7   6   5   4   3   2   1
BVG

FOR
Emma, Lily, and Spencer

*The author would like to acknowledge
Evan Ross, Patricia Ryan, and Lizzy
for their continuing love and support.
Thanks to Jackie Dembar Greene and
Christine Mirabito, who read this book in its early
stages and provided ongoing encouragement.*

chapter 1

My aunt is moving in today. Bones has come over early this morning to have a look at her. We are sitting on the bottom step of my front porch twisting twigs into the dirt by our feet.

"How come your aunt's never been around before?" Bones asks. She scratches her neck and stares down the street.

"Dad says she takes long journeys," I tell her.

"Yeah, but you're supposed to come back." Bones pulls a broken button out of the coffee can next to her. "You know, for important stuff like birthdays and weddings."

And funerals, I silently add.

My mother spoke lovingly about her sister, but I have never met my aunt and when she didn't appear for my mother's funeral, I stopped believing she ever existed. No one else from my mother's side of the family is still alive, but there would be little room for them. My father's family is so fat and so many that they take up all the space for relatives.

"So, your aunt's going to stay with you?" Bones asks. She spreads her lean fingers out in the dirt, making a faint handprint.

"I guess."

"Forever?" she asks, pushing her hair from her eyes.

I shrug.

Bones sighs. She likes to know all the details and gets frustrated with me when I can't provide them. I am eleven and though she is only six months older, she seems years wiser. We both live on this street, Bones at one end of the block, me at the other.

"If she stays here, it won't stop us, though, will it, Sammy?" Bones asks.

I shake my head. We are on a quest, Bones and me. We are searching for just the right magic that will help us recover the spirit of someone lost. Bones has studied these things, so we spend our days pushing trowels deep into the earth, placing important items in empty coffee cans. We have found arrowheads and ancient bottles made of blue and green glass. We have found the missing half to many pairs of earrings. Once we even found a wedding ring.

"What do you think was here before us?" I ask Bones as I watch a neighbor's laundry flutter in the summer breeze.

She closes her eyes. "There was a meadow there,"

she says, pointing toward a crumbling garage. "And it was always green, even in winter. Everyone thought there was something in the dirt. Something so powerful . . ."

I try to imagine the place Bones sees.

"You have to believe that this was sacred ground, Sammy," she says. "That there's still magic buried here."

"Not around here, Bones." I look at the tiny houses with their sagging window boxes.

"Sammy, don't say that!" She pushes my shoulder. "It'll bring us bad luck."

I'm not sure how much more bad luck I can have. I close my eyes. I want to believe with all my heart like Bones does, because if I do, maybe I could uncover the one piece of magic that would bring my mother back. Then, maybe just for a few minutes, I could see her again. I can almost feel the tips of her fingers tracing hearts on my palm.

Bones elbows me. "Open your eyes. I think your aunt's here."

A taxi pulls up in front of our house. It stops, but no one gets out. It sputters and shakes and then gasps for air. Suddenly the doors pop open and out fly large boxes that hit the street but do not spill. A pillow explodes and feathers float silently into the air. Neighbors open their windows.

"Samantha, you all right?" It is Dr. Andrews from the next house, calling down from his second-floor window.

I run to the sidewalk so he can see me all in one piece.

"It's my aunt," I yell up.

The taxi driver starts talking under his breath about God and the Virgin Mary. Bones and I run around trying to catch the pillow feathers. They fly like wispy snow, and as hard as we try, most slide through our fingers. The ones we can hold in our fists we shove back into the case.

My father finally comes down the front steps, pulling up his suspenders. He is as large as a mountain and I imagine he'll just pull the door off the taxi, reach in, and find my aunt.

Even though Dr. Andrews is the oldest person on our block, he comes to help. So does our new neighbor, Ash. We start an assembly line, handing boxes to one another all the way up the stairs into my house. Finally there is nothing left to carry and we all wait. Where is she?

Somehow, in spite of all her things, we have lost my aunt. The taxi drives off. The neighbors go home. My dad is left in the street rubbing his neck, putting his wallet back inside his pocket. He doesn't say anything to me, but he tugs at my shoulder. This is my sign to follow.

"She already takes up too much space," I say, looking at the boxes piled up in the living room.

"Sammy," my father says gently.

"Everything is out of place now." I move the coffee tables back to their original position and replace the cushions that have fallen. I lay my mother's book back on her chair, as if she will return any minute to finish it.

My father takes one last look out the front window, shrugs, and goes into the kitchen.

"You don't think my aunt knows I don't want her to come, do you, Bones? You don't think I somehow made her disappear?"

Bones grabs the coffee can from the bottom stair. She pulls out a dirty broken whistle, a twisted gold wire, and a piece of a cup shaped like a star. "No. We're not that powerful. We haven't found the right magic yet."

I smell toast and my father calls. Bones goes to the kitchen, carrying the rattling coffee can.

I press my face against the screen door to take one last look into the street. Out of the corner of my eye, I see a flicker of blue, but when I turn to stare it's gone, and like before, I am alone.

chapter 2

"So what happened to her?" Bones asks later.

"My dad says she'll show up," I say.

We're sitting opposite each other digging in the yard of one of our neighbors. We have found only bottle caps and curved clear glass. I watch as two giggly, young girls cross the street. They wear matching bright yellow macaroni necklaces that I know they made at arts and crafts camp. Bones and I used to go, but we're too old now.

Bones looks at the next yard over, which belongs to Mrs. Duncan.

"Don't even think about it," I whisper, twisting my trowel in the dirt.

Bones sighs. Mrs. Duncan is a wiry woman with wild gray and white hair. She's lived in that house all her life, and Dr. Andrews can even remember before that when her parents lived there. Whenever we set foot by her fence she comes out with a big pan and spoon and makes a ruckus, like we're dogs to be scared off.

All the other neighbors on the street tolerate our digging. They whisper a little, and sometimes nudge each other as we walk by, but no one really minds us. On hot summer evenings they even stop and look at the treasures we've found. They push the broken pieces around with their fingers and tell us stories about when they were young.

"If we could just get in her yard for a while," Bones says, sifting the dirt through her hand. There are two places in town where we most want to dig. One is Mrs. Duncan's yard, the other is Shadow Lake Park. These two places hold magic.

We know this because we have a friend at the library, Mr. Gold, who lets us look over the old maps of our town. When we go to visit him I watch over Bones's shoulder as Mr. Gold carefully lays the ancient documents out on a long table. Bones winds her fingers over thin lines of streets and rivers. She finds the way so easily. Even when I keep one finger at the end and trace the twisting path with another finger, I still lose my way. It's Bones who guides me back.

On the most ancient map, the one we can look at but can't touch, are tiny drawings and letters. Mr. Gold says the elaborate words come from ancient Greek. The paper is thin, brown, and crumbling at its corners. It shows our neighborhood long before our houses or roads were there. The boundaries are barely visible and the place names unfamiliar. It's on this map that we discovered the Lightning Rocks.

I remember pointing out the two rectangular symbols.

"What are those?" I asked Mr. Gold.

"Oh, those," he said in a very serious, soft voice. "Most people foolishly think they're only rocks."

"They're not?" I asked.

"Legend says that they were forged by the gods. Long, long ago the townspeople would bring their most precious things and bury them at the base of the rocks so the gods would look favorably on them. Grant them wishes."

Bones was all dreamy eyed. I shoved her elbow.

"But," Mr. Gold said, "there are other stories. Stories that very few will repeat."

"Like what?" Bones asked.

"There were those who did not believe in the power of such things," Mr. Gold whispered, leaning close to us. "Such a shame what happened to those people. So horrible. They say if you put your ear to the Lightning Rocks, you can still hear their screams."

I covered my ears. Bones gasped.

"You're teasing us," I finally said.

"Maybe," said Mr. Gold, slowly rolling up the map, "and maybe not."

In real life, the Lightning Rocks are as tall as me, the shape of a shoebox, and as thick as a tombstone.

One of the Lightning Rocks is in Mrs. Duncan's yard and one is in Shadow Lake Park.

We can never go in Mrs. Duncan's yard because she has a slingshot and can hit a cat at fifty yards. We've never actually seen her do this. Once, before my mother died, I met Mrs. Duncan on the street just before dark and she touched my cheek and told me how pretty I had gotten. Now when she sees me, she lowers her head and turns away. Sometimes I whisper hello.

"Hey!" says Bones, waving her hand in front of my eyes. "I've been talking to you."

"Oh," I say. "Just thinking."

"Look!" Bones reaches her thin fingers into the dirt and pulls out a shiny metal piece. She spits on it and wipes it on her jeans. Then she drops it in my hand. "You wear them on the cuffs of your shirt for special occasions like weddings and funerals."

"I know," I say. "But look at the top. It's been smashed."

Bones takes the cuff link and turns it in her hand.

"A lot of the things we find are broken." She frowns. "All the magic seeps out if it's broken." She scratches her head and starts to think of a story because everything we find has a story. "Maybe he wore this cuff link when he asked her to marry him."

I nod. That's a good beginning.

"But how did it end up here in the dirt?" I ask.

"Oh, that's the very, very sad part," she says. Some

of the stories we tell are long and tragic, others are short and silly. It depends on what we find.

By the time Bones finishes her tale, it is getting too dark to see clearly and we gather our things and start for home. I watch Bones as she walks with her head up to the sky, the cuff link jingling in the coffee can. I wipe the dirt off my hands and think about my aunt. I wonder if she is bulky and soft and will squeeze me until I'm breathless. When I look up, Bones is far ahead and I have to work hard to match her long strides.

It is early in the summer. We've only been out of school a week, and it still gets cool in the evenings. I stop to tug at the sleeves of my shirt.

"Bones, wait," I call as I see her start to run to her house.

When I get there I stand on the sidewalk and watch as Bones's mother slips her hand around her daughter's neck and pulls her close for a kiss, leaving a circle of bright red lipstick on her cheek. Bones rolls her eyes.

"Come here, Sammy," her mother calls. She kisses me also and closes me in her arms, then lets me go when I no longer hug back.

I sit on the front stairs of Bones's house and watch them. Since my mother died I can barely breathe around them. I feel like they're part of a special group, that no matter how hard I try, I will never belong to again. I pull up and push down my socks over and over.

Her mother runs her hands through Bones's short, sandy-colored hair.

"Wouldn't she look great, Sammy, if she grew her hair long?"

I shrug and pull at my own reddish brown bangs. I trimmed them only days ago. It looked easy when my mother used to do it. But as I was cutting them, one side kept getting shorter than the other. Bones's mom sneaks a look at them, but when our eyes meet she quickly turns away.

"Oh, Bones, your hands . . . ," she says sighing, staring at her daughter's dirty nails.

I feel badly for her mother, who so wants Bones to show some interest in her appearance.

"Got you a present," says Bones's mom pulling out a dress from her bag. It's pale yellow with tiny flowers. I'm not sure what to say so I just smile. Bones will never wear it. She never wears any of them.

"It's for summer. Do you like it?" her mother asks.

I like the way her mother tries. She always says stuff like "It's for Christmas" or "It's for Grampa's birthday." Some special occasion.

Bones touches the dress. It makes a sound like someone folding paper.

"It'll get softer once we've washed it," says her mom.

I nudge Bones. I want her to say something kind to make up for all the times I should have said something kind to my mother, especially when she bought things I hated. But Bones only shows her mother the cuff link. Her mom nods and pushes the dress back into the bag. She walks into the house.

"It's not so bad, for a dress. It wouldn't kill you to say something nice," I whisper.

"She could look at me for once," Bones says. "Maybe she could try harder to see me." We stand in silence, until Bones offers me the can with the cuff link. "I'll come over early and we'll go see Mr. Gold tomorrow."

I wave goodbye to her mother in the window. She blows me a kiss, which makes me feel safe.

"Do you want to stay, Sammy?" she asks.

I do want to, because her dinners are like paintings on a plate. They're all reds and greens and oranges. Mostly, my dad and I eat things that are already cooked and just need to be warmed.

"I can't tonight," I say, afraid that I stay too often.

She waves goodbye.

On my way home, I hop, skip, or take a giant step, to avoid every crack in the sidewalk. Through open windows, I can see the blue-green flicker of televisions. I like the different noises coming from each house. Someone is arguing over the last piece of cake, someone else is rinsing dishes. A phone rings, but no one answers. I start to drag my heels because I can see my own home now. I sit on the curb and play with the tiny pebbles at my feet. This is the time that I think my mother will shake my shoulder and I'll wake up.

"Come on, Sammy. Get up, it's getting late," she'll

say. When I look at her she will be summer bright, with her blue dress the color of sky.

I'll reach up, grab her, and won't let go.

She'll laugh and say, "What's the matter, silly?"

"Bad dream, just a bad dream," I'll say, sinking into her arms.

"I'm here, aren't I?" She'll stroke my hair and notice the ragged bangs. "Well, what on earth?"

"I ruined them."

"Hmm . . . Well." She'll try not to smile or be too angry. "Don't you worry. They'll grow back."

I'll rub my cheek against her hand.

"Come on, Sammy. Time to go," she says.

"No," I say and I hold onto her, but she starts to slip away. I open my eyes and look out to the dark street. I wait for a few minutes, then finally get up from the curb. Time to go.

As I get close to Ash's house I tiptoe. Bones and I have been spying on him for most of the week. My father said that his aunt left him the house and he's only going to live there a few months and fix it up to sell. He's tried to make a garden in the small patch of land in front; he took away the faded pink flamingo that kids used to coat with toilet paper at Halloween and planted thorny roses.

He has taken down the curtains and cleaned the windows for the first time in years. I have never been able to see into the house before and I pause outside the small gate to look in. On the fireplace mantel not far from where Ash is peeling pieces of browned wallpaper off the wall is a painted wooden mask with triangular eyes and razor-sharp teeth. I want to tell Bones about it tomorrow, but she'll ask why I didn't get a better look. I'll have to tell her that I was afraid. She'll nod because she knows I am not the brave one. I'm always the first one to turn back.

I linger by the fence. There's an overturned bucket not far from the living room window. I could step on it and easily see into the room. I tell myself to go home, but instead I gently push the gate open. I go into the yard, step on the bucket, and pull myself up to look into the window. Ash is standing on a creaky ladder grimacing as he removes the gummy wallpaper. He turns toward me and I almost lose my balance as I duck down.

I wait a moment, then slowly stand up until I can see over the windowsill. Ash is no longer at the far wall and I can't see the mask on the mantel anymore. I raise my head to get a better view.

"Boo!" yells the mask, hovering in the air in front of me. I scream and fall to the ground. As I fly out the front gate I can hear Ash laughing.

I run past my front yard. Instead of flowers, it has a few strands of brown grass and three dandelions. Safe in my own backyard, I lean against the back door to catch my breath before I go inside. I look up to the sky and wish on a star. I used to wish for a million things, but now I only wish for one.

I have forgotten about my aunt. Where is she? I pull at my crooked bangs and sigh.

"They'll grow back," I hear my mother whisper in the night.

My father opens the back door and I tumble into the kitchen.

"Was that you screaming?"

"What?" I stare out into the backyard.

"What's the matter? What are you looking at?" He sticks his head outside.

"Nothing."

"It's dark. Aren't you supposed to be home by dark?"

I look at him in the dim kitchen light and realize he knows nothing about me. The thing that I like most is that he doesn't try to hide this. I should write a list of all the things he needs to know, like my shoe size, my favorite color, all the things that scare me.

He needs to learn to sigh loudly, but not seem too disappointed, while he's holding my report card. He needs to learn to give me a handful of cookies and sit with me at the kitchen table in the late afternoon as if that was the only place he ever wanted to be.

He's changed from his painter's overalls, but there is still a tiny drop of pale yellow paint on his cheek. "Have a seat, please," he says awkwardly, like this was my first time in this house.

I wait for him to speak. He rubs his fingers over the cuffs of his shirt. He's nervous. I'm scared. Has someone else died? But I don't know of anyone else's death that would even matter. Sweat forms on his forehead.

"Sammy," he starts. Then stops. As he bends closer to me I notice for the first time that there is a patch of gray hair above his ear. How old is he?

"Here's the thing . . ."

I have no idea how to make it easier for him to say what he needs to say. I try to be patient, but my arm gets all itchy and my foot starts to twitch.

"Your aunt arrived," he finally says.

chapter 3

"Where is she?" I jump up.

"She's busy," he says. "There's someone here to see her."

"To see her?"

"Sammy, your aunt has a gift."

"For me?"

"No," says my dad, "that's not what I meant. Your aunt is—special."

I stare at him confused. "I'm just going to have a little peek at her," I say. He rolls his eyes and shakes his head.

"Just stay here, please," he whispers.

We sit in the kitchen and stare at each other. He gets a sponge that smells like swampy sneakers and wipes the table with it. I get up from my chair and crane my neck, looking out into the hallway to see if I can find her.

"What's she doing?"

"She's helping someone find something."

"What kind of something?" I ask.

My father shrugs.

"Don't you think I should just say hello?" I quickly sneak down the hallway, not giving him time to answer. Will she have wide, bright blue eyes like my mother and me? Will she have my mother's long, deep laugh? Will she love recipes like mock apple pie and refrigerator cake?

When I look into the living room, my heart starts to beat wildly and my legs quiver. My mother is back.

But as I get closer I realize something is wrong. That's not the way my mother used to sit in that chair. She would dangle her legs over the side, her nose buried in the pages of a well-worn book. I blink to clear my vision.

When I open my eyes, the person who sits in my mother's chair is wearing a dress with a collar so high and so tight that it makes her head look like it just lies on top of her neck, like a ball on a column. I cannot see her legs; they're hidden under the thick, dark, floor-length skirt she wears. Her hair is pulled back so tightly that her cheekbones stick out and shine like glass. She sits with her hands in her lap, both feet on the floor, eyes forward. This is my aunt.

She is listening to a person sitting in a chair that faces away from me. The two sometimes bend together in conversation. The visitor gives my aunt a photograph. My aunt leans back, stares at it, and puts her hand to her forehead. What is she doing? I go closer and closer until the floor creaks, sounding like thunder.

My aunt opens her eyes and looks straight at me. She stands. I expect she'll come to hug me, but she doesn't move. Her mouth is open, and small, horrible gasping sounds escape. I take a step back as she stares at me, like I'm a ghost or someone who can turn her to stone. The woman who has been sitting across from my aunt jumps up and turns to me, panicked.

"She's having a vision," the woman yells. "What do we do?"

I race back to the kitchen and look at my father, who's searching my eyes for some explanation. I run into the pantry and slam, then lock the door. The pantry is a stupid choice because it's cramped and the window only opens about two inches before it slips and bangs closed. I pull the string that turns on the dusty lone lightbulb in the corner. Everything looks slightly yellow.

I touch my face to make sure all seems right. There are noises from outside the pantry. People speaking, doors closing, and then quiet.

I might be able to stay in here for quite a while. The large shelves hold cans of chili and soup and pineapple. There are store-bought cake mixes and little containers of frosting that don't ever go bad no matter how old they get. There are little boxes of cereals, pretzels, and my mother's favorite, candy hearts. My father and I don't eat those. Mostly my father eats canned peaches in heavy syrup. There's one shelf stacked high with them. Late at night he opens a can and adds two scoops of fudge ripple ice cream and a mashed, stale graham cracker.

I sit on the step stool, with my hand on my chin. How did things change so fast? Only a few months ago my mother would come in here and grab the pancake mix or the cereal or the peaches. My mother died very quickly, maybe even in seconds. In the time it takes to reach for a can of peaches, she was gone. She died in a bus accident, riding into town to go to the museum, which she loved.

At the museum, she would sit for hours staring at paintings of gardens. I always got itchy when I went with her. I was much more interested in the one mummy they had in the museum basement that seemed to look worse each time I saw it. Now, I wish I had sat longer with her and stared harder at the paintings to see what she saw inside them.

She was getting off the bus when a truck hit it from behind. I think that if she had just moved a little faster or even a little slower she would be alive now. She would have been safe if she'd gone on Wednesday or Saturday instead of Thursday. I play this game in my head, where I think of the many ways she could have saved herself. Sometimes I can't stop playing it.

My mother read a story to me once, from a religious magazine at the dentist's office, about a little girl who received a miracle. She could change any day out of her life. In the story, the girl chooses something silly like the day she played a trick on her brother. If I could change any day, I would go to the city with my mother that Thursday and I'd make her get off one stop early to go to the little Italian bakery. We'd walk to the museum eating our leaf-shaped cookies. We would see the bus accident.

"Oh, Sammy, weren't we lucky today that we got off when we did?" she would say. "How tragic." She would hold my hand and pull me away. Weren't we lucky today?

On one of the shelves in the pantry, where no one can see, I start to carve my name with an old fork. I hear a knock on the door, but I ignore it. I hear mumbles and another knock. The doorknob rattles.

"Sammy? Come on, Sammy," whispers my dad.

I don't say anything. It's always better not to say anything so they wonder if you're dead or alive.

I hear my aunt knocking. I can tell it's her, because it doesn't have the same force as my father's knock.

"I'm sorry, Samantha. I'm so sorry," she says quietly. "You startled me."

I carve deeper into the wood.

There are no other sounds. I think they've given up on me. I might have to live in here forever with the syrupy peaches and abandoned appliances.

I see the backyard light go on. There is thumping and groaning and my father's face looks at me through the window. Whatever he's standing on can't wholly support him so he steps up and down quickly before he falls through. He reminds me of a horse on a merry-go-round. With each crest he catches a tiny glimpse of me.

When he is satisfied that I am alive, he goes from the window and the backyard light shuts off.

A note is slipped under the pantry door. I refuse to see it, but it has been dipped in a sweet scent that makes me want to pick it up and bring it closer.

Nothing my aunt could ever write will make me leave this room. It is probably a wishy-washy note of apologies. I pick up the envelope and open it. Out slides a picture, or rather half a picture. I hold it close to the lightbulb and try to figure it out. It's a black-and-white picture of two legs—girl's legs. Whoever it is, she is standing in a flowered field. There is something in the background, but it's too blurry to make out. I look in the envelope to see if the other half of the picture is there. No, only a note that reads, "Two halves make one whole."

I open the door a tiny bit and peek through the crack. I don't see my aunt anywhere. I hear a scraping sound and I look down at the bottom of the door. There, at my feet, is a can of sweet rice pudding, my favorite food these days. But we ran out of it yesterday and my father refused to buy more. He is worried about how poorly we eat. I look at the can but do not go to get it. I climb back on the step stool and stare at the photo under the yellow bulb. Who is she? Where will I find her? I hold the envelope up to my face and smell the sweet scent of lilacs. There is a movement by the door and when I look, there are two cans of pudding. I can't help smiling.

"Thank you," I whisper.

Somewhere in the darkness my aunt says, "You're welcome."

chapter 4

"You know," says Bones, "maybe your aunt is a spy or a murderer. She probably just broke out of prison."

We are on our way to the library with our small sack of treasures to show Mr. Gold. I was going to bring the ripped picture to show Bones, but instead I hid it in the top drawer of my bureau. This is something that I want to keep to myself.

"Maybe she's murdered all her husbands. Poisoned them," says Bones, pretending to strangle herself and making gurgling noises. "Late at night, she pours them a glass of—"

"Look." I grab Bones's arm.

We watch as Mrs. Duncan crosses the street two blocks in front of us.

"Spit in my hand," Bones says. "Quick!"

We think it's bad luck to have Mrs. Duncan cross

the street in front of us. I spit in Bones's hand and she says some words that she claims are Latin. We watch as Mrs. Duncan disappears into the darkness of her house.

Bones is usually impatient, but this morning she seems to slow down and try very hard to walk with me, though I think it gives her the twitches. My legs have always been shorter than hers. In the past few months, it has gotten worse as she has grown up toward the sky and I seem to be shrinking toward the earth. I barely come up to her shoulders now, but I have always been the littlest, the one they put up front in class pictures.

"I'm working on a plan of how we can get over to Shadow Lake Park," Bones tells me.

I don't have as much interest as Bones does in the park. It's far away on the side of town where all the troubles seem to happen. My mother mentioned the park a few times, but I don't tell Bones that because I never mention my mother to anyone now.

"In the old days, everyone would pack picnics and lay out their blankets. They'd listen to band concerts," Bones says. "My mother said at night the mist looked like angels dancing on the water."

The Shadows, as it was nicknamed, is an old amusement park, now filled with large rusty things that people have broken and thrown into heaps. The hills were once green, but these days they're sort of an odd yellow. Pieces of broken beer bottles sparkle in the sunlight. The rides that weren't taken apart have rotted into the earth and their sharp metal pieces form weird sculptures across the field. It looks like the ruins of an ancient city. No one goes there. It's too scary.

Bones's uncle, who works for the city, drove us by the Shadows once. He was smoking a cigar and little pieces of it kept spitting out of his mouth when he spoke. He kept telling us all the horrible things that had happened at the park, I guess to scare us off. Some people claimed that creatures came out of the lake, or that the mist captured and dragged lost souls into the water to drown them. Teenagers swore that late at night ghouls had loud parties at the base of the Lightning Rock there.

I remember saying something to Bones's uncle about the Lightning Rocks, but he waved his hand and rolled his eyes.

"I don't believe in that Lightning Rock mumbo jumbo. When people came to town to get supplies that's where they used to tie their horses up. You kids don't know nothing about history." He spit out more tobacco. "Lightning Rocks! Hocus pocus! Bunch of nonsense."

She never said anything, but I could see in her eyes that Bones thought the Shadows was full of magic.

"Do you think your uncle would take us back?" I ask Bones.

"Naw. My mom says he smokes and swears too much. I got another plan."

I get quiet.

"You still want to go, don't you?" she asks me.

"Sure. It's just that it's . . . all the way cross town."

"I think we're meant to go back," she says seriously. "There's something magic there calling."

I feel the same way too, but a small shiver runs up my spine.

She opens the large door of the library and we race each other up the four flights of steps to Mr. Gold's office.

chapter 5

I think he's sleeping when we walk in, but the door creaks and Mr. Gold's eyes pop open. He moves around his desk in baby footsteps to see what we've brought for him. I think he's ninety, but Bones says he must be older.

"Ladies, nice to see you. What have we got today?"

Bones lays the small plastic bag on the counter. It's full of the things from our latest digs. Mr. Gold picks up a matchbox and turns it up toward the light. He adjusts his glasses.

"Ah, the Cloverleaf Club. This place was open when I was a little boy. It's gone now. Look," he says. We stand close to him. Drawn inside the matchbox is a heart with two names inside and the date: 1946.

" 'Ted loves Alice.' Do you think they still do love each other?" he asks, gently placing the matchbox back in the bag. "Such wonderful things you both find," he says, smiling.

I look around Mr. Gold's office. It is a mess of ancient books and well-read journals with pictures of real mummies. Lining the walls are faded color photographs of all the places he has been.

"Isn't it amazing how many things stay buried," he says, "just waiting for someone to find them and bring them into the light?"

Bones says that Mr. Gold's money built this library and in return he is allowed this office. Neighbors say he is very wealthy. I don't know what his money buys because his clothing, though clean, is often missing buttons and worn through at the elbows. He is bony and eats only watercress-and-onion sandwiches and drinks water from light green bottles. There's a rumor that he paid more than a billion dollars for a tiny painting that he keeps buried in a room under his house. We've never seen it.

Mr. Gold picks up the old coin that we found by the fence leading to Mrs. Duncan's yard. Part of it is coated with sap or tar. We were afraid to clean it, in case we rubbed away the surface.

"This is rather fascinating," Mr. Gold says. "Yes, yes." He peers over the tops of his glasses. "We must get the book."

"The book," Bones and I repeat, and march over to the sagging shelf that's covered with crumbling newspapers and photographs of old explorers. I dig out the dusty book with yellowed pages that shows pictures of the fronts and backs of coins. I hand it to Bones. She lays it on Mr. Gold's desk.

"Ready, ladies?" Mr. Gold starts to rub a little at the surface of the coin. He stops and searches through the pages for the right picture. We stick our faces so close to the book that we all breathe the same air. He raises his head and we raise ours. He holds the coin up again and sighs and shakes his head.

Bones frowns. I watch as Mr. Gold fumbles in back of his desk. Things keep falling off the bookshelf, but he doesn't notice. He pours something from an old, ugly bottle into a glass. It fizzes slightly. He drops in the coin. It swirls around for a few seconds and dives to the bottom in a stream of bubbles. He fishes it out with a spoon that he uses to stir his coffee.

He takes an old, soft cloth and wipes the coin. "Well, this is a marvelous find, my friends." He flips the coin in the air and Bones catches it.

" 'One ride,' " Bones reads.

"On Pegasus," says Mr. Gold.

"What's Pegasus?" I ask.

"In Greek mythology, it's a winged horse," says Bones, staring at the coin.

"This Pegasus," says Mr. Gold, "was a roller coaster."

"At the Shadows, right?" asks Bones.

"So you've heard of it, then?" he says excitedly.

"Just a little," she answers.

I shrug.

Mr. Gold raises his arms toward the ceiling. "Pegasus rose out of the ground so high that on warm, rainy days, when you reached the mist at the top, it was like you touched heaven." He pauses. "It's still there at the Shadows, but so sad to see now."

"How come your uncle didn't show us it?" I say, knocking Bones's elbow.

"Many people wouldn't even drive into that part of the park anymore," says Mr. Gold. "I'm surprised you haven't seen more of these." He points to the coin. "There must have been thousands of them."

"Thousands?" asks Bones.

Mr. Gold and I look at each other. Bones slumps in the chair.

"Many places left to dig, my friend." Mr. Gold gently rubs Bones's shoulder. "Many lost things to find. Someday you will find the one thing above all others."

"We'd better go," she says, giving the coin to me. I slip it in my pocket.

"Do you think we could look at the maps again soon?" I ask Mr. Gold. I hope this will cheer up Bones.

"I think I can arrange something," he says, sitting in his chair. The really old map is kept in a special safe down at the bank and can only be removed by him.

"I know that I don't need to tell you," says Mr. Gold, leaning back in his chair, "that there are some places in this city that have fallen into grave disrepair.

These places are dangerous and I know that you'd never take it upon yourselves to go there." He stares at us and suddenly looks like a giant instead of the tiny man he is. "But I don't need to tell you that, do I?"

We both stand there shaking our heads in some direction that means neither yes nor no. Bones starts to tap her shoe.

"Well, we'd better go," Bones says.

"Yup, better go," I say. Bones starts down the stairs.

Outside the door Bones looks at me and wipes her hand across her forehead. I grin.

She says, "I want to go get a book on stars."

I don't ask her why. She has millions of things she wants to learn about.

"I'll meet you on the first floor," I say.

The first floor is the children's room. I don't come in here very much because it always reminds me of all the books I've ruined. I read so slowly that I can't finish any book I start. After a page or two, I put the book on the table by the side of my bed. It ends up on the floor and then it ends up under the bed or shoved between the bed and the wall. When I return it to the library, the pages are buckled and the covers are torn. I think they must have a file on me. I can look through the rows and know the books I've taken out. They never fit back on the shelf right. They can't settle back in with the others.

In the children's room there are three older girls gathered around one of the round wooden tables. They are hiding a very small book inside a very large folder. Every few seconds they open the folder, giggle, and read passages to each other in whispers.

I sit down at the end of the row next to them with my head close to the bookshelf, trying to hear some of what they're saying.

Without warning, the librarian comes over to the girls and snatches the book and folder. "I'll take that, thank you very much," she says.

I stare at the librarian until she looks over her glasses at me. "Yes? Are you party to this?"

I shake my head and tug at a book that has been shoved in backward and upside down. Its pages are twisted and wrinkled. I have to pull hard to get it out.

The librarian watches as the girls pack up their things and leave. She puts the folder in the back room and returns to her desk but continues to watch me. I look at the old book I pulled from the shelf. Its soft pages are crinkled, its corners folded. Have I taken this out before? I stare at the cover. No. Who would have ever taken this one? It has a giant compass on it and the binding is held together by thick black electrical tape that has started to unravel.

"Want that one?" the librarian asks.

I walk up to the counter.

"I don't have my card. Can I still take it out?" I ask.

She raises her head and looks at me over her glasses. "I'm not supposed to let you."

"I know," I say.

"Where is your card? Is it lost?" she asks accusingly.

"Yes, it's very lost," I answer.

"You have to pay for a replacement." She reaches noisily for a huge binder that holds the names of everyone who has ever lost their card.

There are people in line behind me holding their crying children. They sigh loudly. The librarian has misplaced her pen. A round girl is dancing pirouettes across the floor.

"This wouldn't have happened if you hadn't lost your card," the librarian says to me.

"Forget it. I don't really even like to read," I say. The book drops on the floor and I am afraid she'll think I just threw it there. I pick it up, leave the counter, and go sit at the round table. I stare at the north and south on the cover. Good, now I don't have to take it home.

"What's your name?" the librarian asks a few moments later. She sits with me at the table, holding a pencil and a card.

I tell her my name.

"Address?"

"What about the two dollars?" I ask. "I don't have any money."

"I know. I'll consider it an IOU." She continues to check off small boxes and passes me the card to sign.

"For every book you read I'll take a quarter off your bill."

"It might take me forever to pay it off," I tell her. She seems to be thinking it over.

"I'll still do it, if you will," she says.

Now I'm afraid to tell her I don't want the book, haven't ever wanted it. She stamps it and places it in my hands. She looks in my eyes and it seems like she wants to say more to me. I wait patiently because my mother always told me to give people time to put their thoughts together. Suddenly, though, Bones is at the table with a bundle of books.

I don't think Bones has ever read a children's book. Mostly she reads about fossils, bones, and old civilizations. In her room she has one whole shelf filled with books on Egypt.

The librarian seems to know Bones. She looks at the titles and smiles. "There's no stopping you, Victoria."

Victoria. I don't know anyone else who calls her that.

Bones scratches her head and nods to the librarian.

"Can you carry some of these?" Bones asks me. "I have one more I couldn't manage. I'll be right back." She runs out the door.

Someone rings the little bell at the counter and the librarian quickly gets up to help.

"So, we have a deal, don't we?" she says, turning to me.

"Deal," I say, crossing my heart.

I gather everything and wobble out to the waiting area. Bones returns and we check out all her books and put them in her sack. I put my book on top.

"What's that?" she asks.

I roll my eyes. "Some dumb book I had to get."

On the way to Bones's house we pass Dr. Andrews, who still pats us on the head like he did when we were little. In front of Mrs. Duncan's yard Bones starts to slow down. She stops in the shade of one of the old oaks.

"Not here," I whisper to her.

"Just want to look for a minute," she says, putting the sack down. She makes believe that she is re-arranging the books while we sneak peeks at Mrs. Duncan's backyard through the tiny spaces in her fence. I have to turn my head at an odd angle and squint to see through the slats. A window on the second floor of her house opens and Mrs. Duncan yells down in her gravelly voice.

"What are you two looking at?"

Bones slings the sack quickly over her shoulder and we run all the way to her house. I leave her on her front steps.

"I've got to get home for a little while. My aunt and everything. Come over later," I tell her, still trying to catch my breath.

"Sure. Here, don't forget this." She laughs and hands me my book. She looks at the bag of treasures and offers them to me. She is frustrated because they never turn out to be exactly what she wants them to be.

"I'm sorry about the coin," I say, taking the bag. "Someday we'll find something really special, Bones. And it'll change everything."

chapter 6

*W*hen I'm within two houses of mine, I notice an older woman pausing in front of my house. She's carrying a brown envelope close to her heart. She knocks on my door. I can't see who answers, but the conversation is short. She leaves without the envelope but still holds her hand to her heart.

When I open the front door I hear voices coming from the kitchen. I put the book and the bag of treasures on the sofa and tiptoe down the hallway. My aunt is at the kitchen table with my father. I sit down with my back against the wall just outside the kitchen door, straining to hear their conversation. I crane my neck to see my aunt shake her head back and forth. My father is bent over his coffee cup.

"It's starting already, isn't it?" my aunt asks.

"They just ask if this is the house where the finder lives."

"It's amazing how quickly they can find me, but not the item they've lost," she says.

She gets up and rinses her cup in the sink. I move my back tighter against the wall.

"I don't think this job will take long. Just a few more days and I'm sure I'll find what they're looking for," she says. "I can leave after that, before things get too crazy. Thank you for taking me in."

This confuses me. Hadn't she come to take care of me?

"I tried to track you down," says my father. "I feel bad that you found out too late to come for the funeral."

There is a long pause and I wonder if she's still in the room with him.

"I always thought it was better to leave her. She had an opportunity to have a life here."

"You could have stayed, Constance," my father says. "Things would have gotten better."

"I was practically run out of town. Have you forgotten?"

"I haven't forgotten," my father says softly. "Many of those people are gone now."

"Aurora Duncan?"

My father sighs. "Nothing will ever change her."

I try to scoot closer when I hear them talking about Mrs. Duncan.

"It's never brought you happiness, has it, this gift?" asks my father.

"It's always interfered with everything I've loved,"

Aunt Constance says softly. "It's always the same wherever I go. Sooner or later they find me, in whatever town. They knock on my door at all hours holding out their pictures, wanting me to help them. Soon the neighbors start to complain about the stream of people. Eventually I have to move on. It's almost as if I've let their lives become more important than my own. Over the years I found it so hard to continue relationships or have any kind of personal life, even with my own sister, obviously."

"I don't think she ever really gave up on you," says my father. "She knew sooner or later you would find yourself here."

They are silent and I hold my breath.

"Why don't you stay with us for a while?" my father asks. "If you could help Sammy it would mean a lot to me. She's so much like her mother. A lot like you, too, Constance."

Me, a lot like her!

There is a long pause and my father says something I can't understand. He pushes his chair back from the table.

I crawl down the hallway, open the front door, and slam it, as if I've just returned. My father is coming out of the kitchen.

"Hi," I say too loudly. "Are you ready to go?"

On Saturday mornings my father and I go out for pancakes at the diner. He always takes a long shower, puts on a clean shirt, and slaps on pine-scented aftershave. We sit at a large red vinyl booth and he reads the newspaper as I play with the buttons on the jukebox. I like this time, though we hardly speak to each other.

"Well, let's have breakfast here this morning." He motions to the kitchen.

I groan.

"We can't eat out all the time," he says.

"Why not?" I ask.

"Come on." He pushes me gently into the kitchen.

My aunt is cracking eggs into a mixing bowl.

"I was going to scramble some eggs, is that all right?" she asks.

"That would be great," says my father.

I hate eggs and things that look like eggs. Lately I like food that comes out of a can, like spray cheese, something my mother would never let me eat.

I watch my aunt moving back and forth between the cupboard and the counter, looking for all the things she needs to cook with. I should help her find her way, but I don't. Isn't she supposed to know where everything is? I slump down in the chair.

"When are you leaving?" I ask loudly.

My father kicks me under the table.

"I'm just trying to make conversation," I whisper.

He returns to his newspaper. I make soft clicking noises.

"So what kind of job are you doing?" I ask my aunt as she lays the knife and fork next to me.

Oops. They both stare at me, knowing I was eaves-dropping on their conversation.

"It's for someone in town," she says, eyeing my father. My father sighs deeply and looks at me like he's thinking of sending me to Jesus camp.

I stare at my aunt. I guess I should be happy. I didn't want her to come to take care of me, and after she's done with this job, she'll go. I think of the picture she gave me last night. Why give it to me? Maybe she's a lunatic. Maybe she has millions of photographs that she rips in half. Maybe Bones was right, maybe she does poison—

"Juice?" she asks.

I try not to, but I nod. I sit at the table with my head on my hands. It takes me a moment to realize that she has used one of my bedsheets as a tablecloth. She does everything wrong.

My mother always dried the sheets on the line in the sun till they were blue white and thin soft. She would laugh at me when I said I didn't want new scratchy ones. I rub my hand over the edges. My mother had held these corners, though there is no trace of her touch now. I know that someday all the things she washed and dried will be washed and dried by someone else. The fingerprints she left behind, in time, will lie hidden beneath mine, or my aunt's, or my father's. Soon all she was will fade away and there will be nothing left to remind me that she ever lived in this house.

My aunt pushes a plate in front of me. I expect to see a fluffy hill of eggs, but instead there are three pancakes drenched in thick brown syrup with sausages on the side.

I look up at her, but she offers no explanation. She lightly places her hand on my shoulder, but it feels uncomfortable so I shift and make her let go.

My father is devouring his eggs. We eat like pigs. We've been starving.

My aunt sits at the table with us and sips her tea.

"Don't you ever eat anything?" I ask her as I lick the syrup from the corners of my mouth. I sound too harsh.

"I don't have much of an appetite today," she says.

She is very pale and the skin beneath her eyes is dark and wrinkled. It's early in the morning, but already she looks tired.

There's a knock at the door and my father excuses himself to answer it.

"Sammy, about the picture I gave you—" my aunt says softly.

"Was that my present?"

"Well," she says looking as if she's thinking how to explain things. I push the pancakes away. I don't want them anymore. I don't want an aunt who gives me strange things like broken pictures. I want an aunt who plays piano and cheats a little at board games. An aunt who makes popcorn that spills out over the bowl.

My father returns. He shrugs. "Someone selling something." He takes a large sip of coffee and won't look at me.

"I hope you both don't mind, but I thought I'd go have a rest," she says. "I've been traveling for so long."

I wonder what her face would look like if she smiled. Does she wonder the same thing of me? I wash my plate off and set it in the rack to dry.

"Dad, why is she here?" I whisper when she is gone.

He washes his plate in the sink too long.

"I guess she's here to help us find our way," he says.

We weren't lost when my mother was alive. Did she take the map of our lives with her?

"I'm off just for a while," my father says. "Got to give this guy a quote on painting his garage." By summer's end my father's skin will be golden brown from the hours he's spent outside painting houses.

I almost tell him that I don't want him to go because I'm afraid a car or bus will hit him. He'll be gone too, leaving my aunt and me to grow old and ugly in this tiny house.

He looks at me, then asks, "Do you want to come with me?"

"What?" I say loudly. He's never asked before.

He seems shy. "I just thought if you didn't have anything to do, we could—but it's only up the street. Not important." He's already out the door.

I go into the living room and get my book from the sofa. There is something poking out from under the other cushion. I pull it out. It's a photograph of a family I don't know. There is a circle around one of the people in the picture, a young man. Written across the bottom of the photograph is a note:

Please help us find our oldest son.
He left home five years ago.

I wonder how many faces my aunt has seen. How many lost pieces of people's lives has she found?

My father has forgotten something and comes back through the front door. I toss the photograph down and throw the cushions on top of it. I start to run upstairs. He stops me.

"Could you tell me where you're going?"

"Upstairs," I say.

"No, not now," he says. "This morning. I woke up and you weren't in the house."

I shrug. "I always go to the same places."

"I don't know where those same places are, Sam."

I guess it must be hard to have to worry about something that you haven't really worried about before. It's like the sickly dog Bones once owned. She had to take it out for walks and feed it. She had to sleep with it when it howled all night. Sometimes its body heaved and it threw up green stuff all over the sidewalk. Finally her mother said she had found a new home for the dog on a dairy farm. Bones was sad for a day. Then she confessed that she was tired of the dog anyway. It had taken up all her time and become too much work.

I try to need very little from my father.

"Tell me where you're going next time," he says. He grabs his notebook from the hall table and walks quickly out the front door.

"Wait," I say quietly, but when I look out the front window he is already across the street and turning the corner. I always miss my chance to be with him. I take my library book and run up the stairs to my room.

My room is full of heaps of clothes that are either too small or outdated. I cleaned out my closet the day before my mother died. We were going to put all the things I had outgrown in bags to donate to the poor children's home down the street. Instead, they surround me. I kick clothes under the bed; some hang from my desk chair. Many are things she made for me and are now constant reminders of every Christmas, Easter, and birthday with her.

I take a sweater off my floor, one my mother knitted. I roll it into a ball and use it as a pillow. I lie down on the bed and stare at the compass on the cover of the library book.

It's a book on navigation. I start to read it, but I can't even find my way through the first chapter. I let it drop to the floor.

Feeling guilty, I turn and look at it. The back cover is open and there is an old form where children years ago wrote their names when they checked out books. I look down the list of names and stop at the third. It was written so long ago and is smudged and faded; still, it is hers. My mother's name. I rub my eyes and look again just to make sure I'm not imagining things. It's still there. I wonder, did she take this book out for the same reason I did? I pick it up and something falls out from between the last few pages.

It is a faded map of the different areas of Shadow Lake Park. I trace one of the paths with my finger. It leads from the lake, past the Lightning Rock, across the field to Pegasus, the roller coaster. I close my eyes and try to imagine what it must have been like to walk that path with her on a long-ago summer's day.

chapter 7

"Come on, wake up! You sleep too much lately." Bones is shaking me.

"Go away," I say, and turn from her. I pull the covers over my head.

"I have something for you."

I peek out.

Bones is staring at my room. At her house everything has to be off the floor and put away. She starts to scratch her arms and jiggle her leg. Slowly, as if I won't notice, she casually gathers clothes off the floor and folds them.

"Is it a large, expensive something?" I ask.

She can't answer. I know she's thinking of ways to reorganize my room. I see her planning, finding perfect locations for bookcases and shelves. I feel for the map under my pillow. I was going to give it to Bones as a present, but part of me wants to keep it quiet, not tell anyone. I slip the map into my pillowcase.

"Come on, let's go outside." I throw the covers back.

"Okay," Bones says. She stops, but it's hard for her to leave something undone. As she goes, she picks up a pair of jeans and drapes them over my desk chair.

Outside, we sit on the front steps and she digs out a small bag of crushed cookies from her front overall pocket. She dangles them in front of me. Her mom stops at the fancy bakery at the end of the week and they give her the broken pieces of thick sugar cookies. Bones drops the bag in my lap. She takes out a folded piece of paper. It is a map she's made of our town.

"Where are we?" I ask.

Bones points to a small X at the bottom right of the paper.

"Where's the Shadows?" I ask.

She points to another location on the top left of the paper.

"Could we walk?" I ask.

She shakes her head.

"It goes through a kinda rough part of town. We really need to take a bus to the other side."

"I don't want to take the bus, Bones."

She doesn't say anything else to me. What if she wants to leave me behind so she can go forward? I guess I can't blame her.

I think back to the time we first met. No one liked Bones. She never spoke to anyone, not in school, not ever. Everyone told lie-filled stories about her. They said her brain was deformed because she ate shiny green paint chips. She did little to prove them wrong.

Once I forgot something at school and ran back inside long after classes were done. I barged into the classroom and found Bones speaking to a teacher who taught much older kids. He was checking over a paper she had written for him. They both stared at me for a moment but then returned to their conversation, most of which I couldn't understand. I thought she was always quiet because she didn't know anything. I realized then that she was quiet because she knew everything.

She was the only other kid my age on the block. My mom would tell me to go talk to her, make friends with her. "Ask her over, Sammy." But I never would.

Then Bones missed weeks of school and one of the teachers asked if I would drop some things off at her house.

"You live on the same street, don't you?"

I dawdled, but when I finally went by her house, I didn't even knock. I just left the books on the steps. As I turned away Bones's mother opened the door.

"I just left these, from school."

"Want to come in?" she asked.

"No, thank you."

She nodded as if she'd known that would be the answer. She closed the door and as I left I looked into their small front yard. It was full of fist-size holes. I ran home but realized later that I had left my report with Bones's stack of work. I would have to redo it if I didn't go back to get it.

I hoped her mother would just open the screen door and hand me the paper, but when I got to their house Bones was digging in the dirt in the front yard. With filthy hands she held out my report to me.

"You must have wanted to come back," she said, kicking at the dirt.

"What?"

"If you leave something behind, you'll come back for it."

"It was an accident," I said.

"It was fate," she said.

"What are you doing?" I asked.

"Digging."

"How come you don't come to school?" I asked. "Are you sick?"

She sat down on her front step and looked down the road as if she could see another town from here.

"My father called to say that things had changed for him and he was coming to get us. Said he had a house with an endless porch all picked out." She wiped the dirt from her hands. "I didn't want to miss him. He said he'd be here soon."

I looked up the street. There was no one in sight.

"But he hasn't come," she said softly. She got up and went back to digging. I had my school report in my hand. There was a small fingerprint on the corner of the paper.

"Sorry," she said as she saw me trying to brush it off. I shrugged.

"You know, there are no two fingerprints alike." She stared into the dirt.

"What are you digging for?" I asked, moving closer to the holes.

"Magic," she said.

She waited for me to walk away, but I didn't. Even though she turned her back to me, I still saw her drying her eyes with her dirty shirtsleeve.

"So, did you find any?" I whispered.

She was quiet for a while, but then she handed me a small shovel. "Want to help me look?"

The next morning I went to her house. Her mother let me in and led me to Bones, who was sitting in her room reading. I dragged her out into the morning and walked with her to school. That afternoon and almost every one since, we've dug into the earth, even on cold days when the ground is frozen and the surface hard to break. We never grow bored with it. It is always what we're just about to find that makes us want to look more.

Bones nudges me from my thoughts and I turn and stare at the map in her hands.

"The bus is the only way to get there, Sammy," she finally says.

"Can't we take a taxi or something?"

"I don't think we can even afford the bus. We'd have to save up another three months for a taxi," says Bones. "We'd be back in school—"

She's not whining, because Bones never whines. She squints as if counting the days and the months in her head.

"I'm too impatient to wait, Sammy."

"You could go without me," I say, though of course I don't mean it.

"I could, I guess," she says very seriously.

I push her off the steps and into the dandelions. She laughs and brushes herself off.

"Hey, who's that?" she asks.

We watch as a girl crosses the street and checks the number of my house. She stands right in front of us and stares as if Bones and I are invisible. I thought she was my age, but now that she's closer I realize she is older. A breeze presses her dress tightly to her body and I notice that there's nothing to her. She is a skeleton.

"Are you looking for something?" I ask.

"Is someone named Constance here?"

"Why?"

"Well, I've lost something really important," she says. "I've looked everywhere and I can't seem to find it. I heard she can find lost things." I want to tell her she'll have to get in line.

"Well, how's she gonna do that?" Bones asks.

"You show her a picture or let her touch your hand and she goes into a trance." The girl lights a cigarette. "That's what I was told."

Bones turns to me, her eyes open wide as if to ask if this is true. All I can imagine is my aunt with her eyelids fluttering and her head twitching as she sits in my mother's favorite chair.

"You must have the wrong house," I say, tired of the strange people who come and knock on the door. "There isn't anyone here like that."

The girl knows I am lying. She stubs out her cigarette beneath her shoe and takes some money from her purse and places it in my hands. "Is that what you need?" she asks.

I hold the bills for a few moments and think, Yes, that's what I need. All I can picture is that taxi ride to Shadow Lake Park to see the Lightning Rock. Bones stares at me. There is probably enough here to pay at least half the trip, but the girl ruins everything by looking in my eyes. She is desperate.

"Here," I say, handing back the money. "Maybe you could try back later."

She puts the money back into her purse. I know she's disappointed. Bones leaves me on the step with her and disappears into my house. The girl makes me nervous. I look around for some familiar face from the neighborhood, but the streets are empty, the houses quiet, like a ghost town.

"Can you do it too, find things?" she asks. I wish she wouldn't give me the chance to lie.

"No," I say finally. "I'm the one in the family who loses things."

She pauses. "Me too."

Bones returns with a glass of water and some saltines and offers them to the girl. She drinks the water, but she won't touch the saltines, even though I know she would like one.

"They're real fresh," I say. I hate the ones that are soggy and feel like oatmeal in your mouth.

She says no, and refuses to look at them. She puts the glass on the step, barely waves, and walks away. Her arms are stiff and her legs are brittle.

"If she ever falls down, she'll break into pieces," Bones says.

We watch the girl turn the corner and drop off the face of the earth. I want to run after her, pull her back, and tell her to wait. Somehow I know she won't return.

"Does your aunt really do that, find things?" Bones asks, popping a saltine in her mouth.

"I don't know. I guess." I think of the picture I found under the sofa cushion. My aunt probably has boxes containing pictures of lost people and things.

"Maybe she could find me something valuable," says Bones.

"Like what?" I ask softly.

"I don't know," Bones says. "Even an arrowhead would be nice."

"How about your dad?" I ask.

"There are just some things you shouldn't go looking for, Sammy."

chapter 8

"Any diamonds?" Bones's mother asks us as she drops the grocery bags at our feet.

We have been sitting here on Bones's top step all afternoon, cleaning the dirt off our latest finds.

Bones lets her mother push the hair out of her eyes. It reminds me of my mother's touch and how effortlessly she could coax me to slip my hand into hers. She could easily embrace anyone, adjusting to fit perfectly into their arms. I wonder if I'll fit better with age. I always seem to bend the wrong way when I reach for someone. I bump heads, I'm clumsy about letting go. I lean too far, or not far enough.

"You're both filthy. Promise me you're not going into anyone's yard without permission. Tell me there won't be trouble. Cross your hearts."

"Oh, Mom," Bones says.

"I worry about my girls," she says, going into the house. "Oh, I forgot, I got these back." She throws a packet of photographs into Bones's lap.

Her mother made us pose for her a few weeks ago so she could use up the film in her camera. Bones takes out the three pictures of the two of us. They are goofy shots with most of our limbs out of the camera's range. I look through the rest of the pack and find one that I can't put down.

"That's weird," says Bones, looking over my shoulder.

It is a picture of only my legs. The top half of me is missing. I stare at my knobby knees and thin ankles and the way I curve my feet. My skinny legs look exactly like the legs in the picture my aunt gave me.

"I've got to go home, Bones," I say, and hand the photograph back to her. As I walk away, she starts to call to me, but I don't answer.

I'm scared to talk to my aunt. When I get home, she's sitting in the kitchen knitting. I run upstairs to get the photograph she gave to me the first night she arrived. I pull it out from the drawer and stare at it. Then I put it back and pile socks on top of it. Sitting on my bed and staring at the dresser, something catches my eye in the corner of the room, a flicker of blue. I turn to look, but it's gone. I rub my eyes, pull the black-and-white picture out, and go back downstairs to sit with my aunt at the kitchen table.

I watch her work the knitting needles back and

forth, but looking closely, I notice many mistakes in the piece. There are clumps of yarn and missed stitches. Some pieces hang down and connect to nothing.

"What are you making?" I ask.

"A sweater."

"Oh," I say.

"If it were Tuesday, I would have said a scarf."

"What is it on Friday?"

"Mittens," she answers.

"Do you ever really make anything?"

"No, I'm not very good at it, but you're the first one that's ever noticed. They"—she motions to the outside—"seem to find comfort in it."

"You mean when they come to see you?"

She nods. "I think it relaxes them. They don't really notice that it doesn't make sense. They watch my hands. I think it helps them to talk, to remember."

There are times when she tricks me and is so perfectly my mother. I slowly move my arms and show her the picture. I push it toward her. She picks it up.

"Ready?" she asks.

"I'm not sure," I say. "It's a picture of my mother, isn't it?" The word *mother* cuts into the back of my throat. I have thought that word every day but have not said it for so long. "I don't know how I know that."

"It's your mother," she says.

"But why would you rip the picture in half?" I ask angrily.

"I didn't rip it in half. She ripped it in half."

My aunt leaves the table and goes upstairs. She is so odd, I wonder if she's going to return, or if that is the end of our conversation. Minutes later she sits back down next to me holding a pink jewelry box. The satin on top is peeling and the velvet sides are threadbare.

"What's inside?" I ask.

"Well, once it was full of sorrows. That's when I saved pictures of boys who never loved me as much as I loved them. Then it was full of dreams; it was where I put my passport and maps of foreign countries."

The box isn't locked, but it's difficult for her to open. Finally the clasp pops and she gently pushes open the top. My aunt smiles at the tiny ballerina in a frayed white skirt. She turns the key in back and the ballerina slowly dances.

"Now I guess it's just for memories," my aunt says, returning to her knitting.

When I look in the box there is nothing there.

"I have looked for the other half of that picture for so long and in so many different places. You see, it's buried somewhere in a box just like this."

She wipes the strand of hair from her cheek and leans back in her chair.

"From a very early age I could find things: rings, misplaced items, pieces the dog had stolen and buried in the yard."

"How do you do it?"

"I don't know. I really don't know. I wish I could

say it was an answer to a prayer. Sometimes it is not so much a gift as it is a curse." She rubs her watery blue eyes.

"How can it not make you happy?" I ask. "I would give anything to be able to do something like that."

She lays her knitting on the kitchen table. "I would give anything to settle down, to not have neighbors complain about the endless stream of people who come to my door. To not always have to look at their pictures or listen to their stories."

"What do they talk about?" I ask.

"They tell me about the ones that are lost: brothers, sisters, high-school sweethearts. All these stories that they've kept inside."

I think of all the things I keep away from others and save for myself. I think of my mother. All of her is now held inside me, someplace in the quiet. I don't know how to let her out. But if I never mention her, how is anyone to know how important she is?

"And the picture?" I ask.

"My sister and I would play a game. She would hide things, and I would never be able to find them. If I did find them it was pure luck." Constance laughed.

"Really?"

"Really, my power didn't work with her. At first it made me so angry, but as we grew, I realized she was the only one that I could be at peace with. She didn't care if I had special powers or not. She only needed me to be a sister." She took a long pause before continuing.

"When we were young, I found some of the things she hid. But," she says, running her fingers along the frayed edge of the picture, "not this. I figure it's not mine to find."

"Don't you have any clue?" I ask.

"She put the top half of the picture in a jewelry box just like this one," she says, gently rubbing her fingers over the corners. "Then she hid it. She was eleven at the time, and I have looked for it ever since. She said she would write me a clue, but she never gave it to me."

I touch the box and imagine what my mother would put inside.

"I have turned over acres of earth," she says. "I just thought in all your travels, you might come across it."

"You used to dig?" I can't imagine her fingers in the dirt.

I look at the black-and-white picture in my hands. I want more than anything to find the other half. I want more than anything to see her face.

"What else is in the box?" I ask.

"I don't know what else is inside. Maybe nothing." My aunt gets up and closes her jewelry box.

"What happened with you and Mrs. Duncan?"

"That was a long time ago, Sammy."

"Tell me, please."

She walks over to the sink and runs a tall glass of water. "I had helped to find some boys from another town who were missing. Though I had tried to keep my gift a secret, people found out and came to me. Do you know Dr. Andrews, Sammy?"

"Sure."

"He asked if I could help him find his pocket watch. He had lost it years earlier. It had been his father's and he hoped I could tell him where it was."

"And?"

"I was pretty sure I knew where it was, but I didn't tell him."

"Why not?"

"I had a feeling it was buried in Mrs. Duncan's yard," she said, turning around and staring at me.

"In her yard?"

Aunt Constance nodded and looked out the window. "Maybe someone stole it, then threw it over the fence. I didn't know how it got there. I only knew that's where it was, so I went to visit Aurora Duncan."

"What happened?"

"I told her about my suspicions and she said that if I went anywhere near her yard or even told anyone what I suspected that she'd have me arrested."

"She couldn't do that!"

"She and her family were well respected in this town then. Anyway, I never told, but she started to make up stories about me. It became harder to stay here any longer."

"Didn't you tell anyone else about Dr. Andrews and the pocket watch?"

"No. I didn't mention Dr. Andrews. I didn't want Mrs. Duncan to spread stories about him." She sat down next to me at the table. "The only person I told about it was your mother. We always joked that we'd go digging in Mrs. Duncan's yard. See what we could find."

I am so close to telling her about Bones and me planning to dig there, but I'm afraid I'll mess things up for Bones, who so wants a treasure. My aunt is gazing at me. She runs her bony fingers through my uneven hair.

"You have the most beautiful blue eyes," she says, rubbing my cheek. "You're so much like your mother that it's alarming."

"You too," I whisper.

"I was wrong to stay away, Sammy. I should have come back. Your mother was so full of life I thought she would be the one to leave, not me. But she found all the things she wanted right here."

My father comes in bringing a sloppy square pizza, which we eat out of the box.

Later, sitting on the front steps watching the fire-flies, I ask him where he goes each morning before dawn. What could possibly need painting at that time?

"Just doing a little extra work, helping someone out," he says.

"What kind of house is it?" I ask. I want to show interest.

"Actually, it's not a house."

"What is it?"

"A garden," he says.

I ask more questions, but he shrugs and says, "It's nothing, nothing at all."

chapter 9

"Don't push!" I whisper. Bones is trying to see into Aunt Constance's locked bedroom.

"What do you think she keeps in there?" Bones looks through the small keyhole.

"Sammy?" calls my father from downstairs.

I shove Bones out of the way as I get up to answer him.

"Yes."

"The sun's out. What are you doing in the house?" he asks me from the bottom of the stairs.

"Nothing."

"What are you girls up to?" He starts to climb the steps.

"All ready," Bones says, as if we were heading somewhere. She slings the sack over her shoulder and pulls me down the stairs with her. "Be back soon," I yell to him as we squeeze by.

He lets Bones run out of the house, but he stops me.

"I was talking to Ash, the man who moved into the house up the street," my father says.

"Oh?" I look down at the paint stains on my father's shoes. I remember the night I looked into Ash's window.

"He's got a bunch of old magazines out on the curb. He said you could look through them if you want."

He lets me pass and I am almost free. Almost.

"People are starting to complain, Sam. You've got to stay out of their yards."

I nod and run outside, looking for Bones. I see her, already in front of Ash's house.

"Come on, Sammy," she says, waving to me.

"You must be Sammy. I'm Ash," he says, holding out his hand for me to shake. He is taller in the daylight. I try not to look into his eyes and he doesn't say anything about the other night. He points to the magazines.

"You can choose what you want, I don't need them anymore. They were up in my aunt's attic. Some of them are pretty old."

They smell musty. Their pages are damp and cling tightly to each other. Bones starts to lay them in the sun to dry out. "These are great!" She shows me their covers. There are pictures of mummies and two-headed babies, haunted houses and zombie frogs.

Ash sits down and starts to pull a few weeds from the garden. His muscular arms are slightly sunburned.

"What do you think?" he says, pointing to the house. "Does it look any better?"

"Are you going to sell it?" I ask.

"I think so, though I'm getting kind of attached to it. I grew up a few towns over, but I left when I was young. My parents moved so I wouldn't get into any more trouble."

"What do you mean?"

His clear eyes look way past me. "Aah," he says, throwing his hands up in the air. "Nothing."

Bones has found an article on a mummy who comes to life every full moon.

" 'He wears a blue amulet around his neck,' " she reads, " 'that starts to glow as he rises from the crypt.' Now, that would be something to find." She searches the article to discover where the mummy was from, but it just says Angel Falls.

"Actually a lot of these stories say Angel Falls," Bones says, thumbing through the pages. "You don't think they just make these stories up?" Ash is about to say something, but he looks at the two of us and the treasure sack by our feet.

"They probably don't list the real city because they don't want to alarm the people who live there," he says.

I help him pull the few remaining dandelions.

"Do you want to see the mask?" he asks.

"Sure. I'm sorry about the other night, I didn't mean to—"

"That's okay, but you should be careful about whose yard you go into."

He runs into the house and returns with the mask. He hands it to me.

"Where'd you get it?"

"Sent away for it from the back of a magazine. It belonged to an honest-to-god Zulu warrior," he says, half laughing. "Cost me five dollars and fifty bubble gum wrappers."

"Hey, Bones, look!" I hold it up.

Bone looks up at Ash and then back down.

"Hey, is this you?" she asks, holding up the page of an old scrapbook and pointing to a yellowed newspaper clipping.

"Where'd you get that?" Ash asks.

"It was in that pile with everything else."

"I didn't mean for that to get there." Ash tries to pull the book from Bones.

"I'm reading it," she says, tugging back.

I put the mask down and sit next to Bones, leaning over to read the article. There is a picture of two boys who are a few years older than we are. They look tired and dirty and their arms are bandaged. One of the boys is Ash.

"You ran away?" I ask.

Ash rolls his eyes. "I went to a tree house that we built. Everything would've been fine. Well, except there was a storm."

"Stop moving it. I can't read what it says," I say to Bones.

"Asher!" someone screams.

Bones slams the book shut as she sees the shadow of Mrs. Duncan loom over us like afternoon shade. We sit at attention.

"This your cat, Asher?" Mrs. Duncan asks in her cranky, loud voice. Scratching sounds and frightened meowing come from inside the large, sagging box she carries. I close my eyes, wondering what she's done to the cat, as Ash goes to open the box.

"Don't do it," Bones whispers.

I imagine Ash looks into the box and then runs screaming down the street while Mrs. Duncan stands there cackling. I open one eye and watch as the cat shakes itself, jumps out of the box, and runs into Ash's house.

"Keep him from scratching around in my yard." She waves her finger.

Mrs. Duncan picks up one of the magazines. She has to squint to see the words, but when she does she throws it back down on the ground.

Looking at me, she says, "God help you, Samantha, what's to become of you now? Your aunt Constance is back, I hear."

Ash whispers, "Constance?"

"God knows it'll be raining frogs next." Mrs. Duncan shakes her head back and forth. "And digging all over kingdom come. What on earth are you looking for?"

"Treasures," I say. "Something magical."

She is motioning with her hands now and raising

her voice. "Magical? Ugh! You'd think your father would have a little better sense than to let you roam the neighborhood."

She takes a long breath.

"Best thing they could do for you is sign you up for Jesus camp. Get you away from your aunt and that one," she says, pointing to Bones. Bones raises her head and glares at Mrs. Duncan.

"Leave her alone," I yell, scaring myself with the size of my voice. Bones's eyes open wide. Ash tries to usher Mrs. Duncan out of his yard. Neighbors stop their chores. I can see their heads turn in our direction.

Someone reaches for my shoulder. I think it is Bones and I push her hand away, but Mrs. Duncan stops, as does Ash, to stare at the person behind me.

"Is there a problem?" Aunt Constance asks.

I am so surprised to see her in the sunlight that I don't answer. Mrs. Duncan starts to inch away.

"Nice to see you again, Mrs. Duncan," says Aunt Constance.

"Constance," Mrs. Duncan says stiffly.

There is a long moment when we all stare at each other and no one speaks.

"Well, I should be going," says Mrs. Duncan finally. Ash closes the gate as she passes through. She leans over the fence, holds onto his sleeve, and pulls him close. "Make sure that cat stops scratching in my yard, Asher."

He watches Mrs. Duncan walk away. In the

distance Bones's mother calls for her to come home. "Oh," Bones sighs.

"And you must be Bones," says Aunt Constance, offering her hand for Bones to shake. "It's nice to finally meet you."

"Nice to meet you," Bones says to Aunt Constance.

Bones's mother calls again. "See ya later," Bones says to me. "Got my uncle's birthday party." She drags her heels. "You better go wash, 'cause she touched you," she says to Ash as she passes him.

"Mrs. Duncan?"

"Yeah, you gotta go wash before your arm starts to shrivel up."

As Bones walks down the street she yells for me to take the magazines home so we can read them later. Ash looks at me and starts to speak too quickly. "You shouldn't pay much attention to Mrs. Duncan, Sammy. She's like that with everyone. You know, every other Wednesday morning she visits her mother in the city. She takes the same train I do, but she ignores me. It's just as well because all she does is complain for the whole ride."

Ash lends me an old red wagon with a twisty wheel that he found in the basement. I pack the magazines on it.

"Do you remember me?" he finally asks Aunt Constance.

"Of course I do," she says gently. "The tree house, wasn't it?"

"You two know each other?" I ask, but they have forgotten that I am here.

"Do you live here now?" he asks her.

"No, not really. This was your aunt's, wasn't it?" Aunt Constance says, pointing to the house.

"She left it to me. I'm thinking of selling it."

"Oh, I see," she says.

"So, you two know each other?" I ask very loudly, trying to catch the magazines that are sliding off the wagon.

"Actually, we've never met before," he says, turning to me.

"So how do you know each other?" I ask, confused.

Ash lowers his head, but I still see him blush. "Well." He clears his throat. "Constance saved my life."

chapter 10
ᥬᥬ

"Tell me again," I say to Bones.

"I told you five times." It is late in the afternoon and Bones and I are sitting in my room looking over Ash's magazines.

"Well, tell me just once more."

"The article said the boys had run away from home to their secret tree house. Lightning struck a branch of the tree and split it. They tumbled down. The tree house and branch fell on top of them."

"And what did it say about Aunt Constance?"

"It just said that the police were very thankful to a young girl, Constance Goodwin, who provided them with extremely helpful information," Bones says as if she were reading it off the paper. Ash took back the scrapbook, even though I tried to sneak it on the wagon with the magazines.

"She saved his life."

I lay back with my head propped up by an old sweater. Bones returns to reading. She does not seem to mind my messy room now. The magazines are all she wants to focus on. She reads each one all the way through, stopping only to tell me a few facts about the tiny people who live in the rainspout in Angel Falls.

I turn on my side. I have been drawing complicated flowers on the street map Bones made. The stems of the flowers run into the lines of the neighborhood.

Bones looks over my shoulder.

"You're good at that," she whispers, then returns to the magazine.

"I know something you don't know," I say.

She rolls her eyes as if to say that's not even possible.

"Mrs. Duncan goes to visit her mother every other Wednesday morning."

"How do you know that?" She drops the magazine.

"Ash told me she takes the same train as he does and he sees her every other Wednesday."

"Are you positive?"

I shrug. "Positive as I can be."

"That's only a few days away," she says.

"You should call your mom, it's getting late."

"I will in just a minute. Can you check with him tomorrow and see if this is the week she goes to the city?"

"Yeah, I guess."

"Sammy, it would be great if we could get into her yard for even an hour!" she says.

"If she ever catches us, she'll kill us. She really will, she'll peel our skin off."

"She won't catch us."

Later when it's dark, I go downstairs to get snacks. I call Bones's mother and say I think Bones will be staying the night. She asks me how I am doing. I say that I'm fine, thank you for asking. She says that she cares very much about me and if I ever want to, I can come over and just talk. I start swallowing too much because I'm afraid she'll start to tell me how much my mother loved me. But she only tells me to remind Bones that she has to be home early in the morning.

I wish Bones would be a little kinder to her.

I look outside into the night. I cross my fingers and promise to always be kind and helpful and patient. I wait for some magic puff of smoke, then the reappearance of my mother. She would shake out her hair, slump into the chair, and say, "Well, that was quite an adventure."

But nothing is there. I can smell turpentine and I realize that my father is now sitting at the kitchen table. I don't know how long he's been there. He pours himself a large glass of milk and dunks cookies into it. I look at his hands. No matter how many times he washes them, there's always paint in the creases of his fingers. He pours another glass of milk and turns to me. "Care to join me?"

Bones is upstairs immersed in another magazine and as yet hasn't cared that I'm not there. I sit with my father. He's reading the paper, but not really. I'm reading a magazine, but not really. He sneaks peeks at me as I look at the pictures.

"Any good?" he asks.

I feel like a doll sitting beside him. His arms are three times the size of mine. His face is filled with scrambly lines.

"Oh, yeah," I tell him. "This is a really good issue."

My pockets are filled with sharp, lumpy things from our digs. I can't seem to rearrange them comfortably. I reach in and empty them onto the table. My father catches a coin that scrambles toward the edge. He stares at it.

"Where'd you get this from?" he asks.

"We found it a few days ago down the street by Mrs. Duncan's fence." I wonder if he'll be mad because we found it by digging in someone else's yard. "It's—"

"I know what it is, it's a ride on the great Pegasus, best roller coaster in the world. I used to collect these things."

"You had a coin collection?"

"Well, no," he says, shifting in the chair. "I used to really collect them at the roller coaster. I worked at Pegasus in the summers at Shadow Lake Park."

"Really?" For the first time I am truly impressed with my father.

"Sure. Everyone worked the park in the summer. Your mother did too."

I thought we had a silent understanding that neither one of us was to ever mention her again.

"Those were great summers," he says, flipping the coin in the air. "You would have loved it there. I bet you'd take right after your mother. You'd ride that roller coaster forever, just like she did."

I'm someone who throws up on elevators. I am going to tell him this, but I want to be my mother's daughter in his eyes. I want to be brave. How many times did she ride it? I want to ask him, but I'm afraid of talking about her.

"Bones and I think a lot about the Lightning Rocks," I say.

"They still call them that?" My father raises his eyebrows.

"Did people bury things at the one in Shadow Lake Park?"

"Sure. I saw them do it."

"You did?"

"I used to have to stay late at the park. The machine room was underground, beneath the roller coaster, and I had to go down there and make sure all the power was off at closing time. When I left the park, I'd always see someone at the base of Lightning Rock kneeling down in the dirt."

"They're magical," I say softly.

"Oh, Sam, I think there was greater magic in that old roller coaster, Pegasus." A smile passes over his lips. "You know, it's still there in the field. I think they're afraid to tear it down." He stops talking and stares at the coin in his hand. He is somewhere else in time. "I loved those summers so much. Your mother and I used to steal away to the machine room under the coaster for a kiss."

He lowers his head.

"Can I keep this, Sam?" he asks.

This is the longest conversation we have ever had.

"Sure," I say.

He closes the coin tightly in his hand.

chapter 11

When I return upstairs, Bones is snoring lightly. She sleeps fitfully, twitching every few moments. I pull the magazine from her hands and cover her with my sheet.

I start my nightly ritual: before my father goes to sleep I go into his room and collect something of my mother's. We haven't given away anything that belonged to her.

I tiptoe down the hall and into my parents' room. The tiny light next to her side of the bed is on, like she was just there. I notice, though, that there is more and more of my father and less and less of her now. I smell pine-scented aftershave instead of the sweet rose powder she used to sprinkle on her skin. Lipsticks, thin tubes of makeup, and tiny perfume bottles lie on their sides on her bureau. I put them upright, though tomorrow they will have fallen again. I imagine my father lines them up each night like dominoes; he pushes one and watches as the others fall against each other. Maybe that is his nightly ritual.

Yesterday I noticed a large brown box in back of the closet. Even though it looks heavy, I can easily lift it. I carry it into my room. I shine my desk lamp on my mother's handwriting on top of the box. It says "masterpieces." I expect it to be the many postcards she got from favorite museum shows. I expect to see fields of flowers or the sea at night. Inside the box are different folders for each year of my life. Inside the folders are Mother's Day cards, tiny construction-paper hearts, and crayon portraits with black yarn for hair. These are the many things I made for her. She even saved my pictures of squiggly red lines and tiny handprints in yellow paint on black paper. Some were not presents. Those had thick creases where I crinkled them up and tossed them away into the trash. She rescued them and added them to this collection.

I look through each piece. At the bottom of the box is a small white envelope addressed to Constance. It's from my mother; I recognize her handwriting. I bite the edges of my fingernails. Should I open it? It is sealed. Maybe she really meant to write Samantha on the envelope and got confused. Very slowly and carefully I start to tear it open. Inside is a small piece of paper.

My aunt is softly knocking on my door. "Everything okay?"

"Sure." I throw the envelope under the bed.

I start to gather all the pieces of art. My aunt enters and silently helps me put the pieces back into their folders and the folders back into the box. The brightly colored string of a necklace snaps and little pieces of macaroni spin wildly around the floor. As I gather them, my aunt holds out her hand and I place them in her palm.

"Couldn't you have saved her?" I ask my aunt.

"I can't save people. I can only find them, Sammy."

She waits for me to say more, but I turn from her and put the last piece of artwork back into the box. She finally whispers, "Good night," and walks out of the room.

As soon as she closes my door, I reach for the envelope under the bed. I pull out socks, shirts, and pieces of jigsaw puzzle. When I finally find the envelope, I pull out the paper inside and look at it under the light. I read it twice softly to myself. It is some kind of poem.

> *Go to the one that carries the Lightning*
> *Go to the place that holds all the power*
> *Count seven steps*
> *There I will be*
> *I wait for you hour by hour.*

When I hear my father coming up the stairs, I put the poem in my drawer and scramble into bed.

I toss and turn, half hoping that Bones will wake

up. She doesn't. I lie in the darkness and try very hard to remember every word my mother ever said to me. This usually calms me. Lately, though, when I close my eyes I see her face, but I get scared because it starts to disappear too soon. I stretch my arm out to capture her, but she fades and I can't get her back from the shadows.

I pull the covers over my head then toss them off completely. I get up for a glass of water. I walk down the hallway and stop when I see my aunt's door open. It's almost always closed. I peek in and see her in the dim light restringing the macaroni necklace. I forget about the water and return to my room and my bed.

Bones is awake and confused.

"Who was here?" she asks.

"What do you mean?"

"I swore someone just shook my shoulder and whispered, 'Get up.'" She pulls off her socks and overalls. I tell her to come to bed. She lies next to me, staring up at the ceiling.

"Oh, I'll never get back to sleep now," she says with a sigh.

I'm secretly happy to have the company. She takes a magazine from the floor. I tell her to read a story out loud.

"Here's one," she says, propping up the pillow. "The ghost boy of—"

"Let me guess," I say. "Angel Falls?"

She nods. It is a long story about the ghost of a young boy who haunts a small town. Bones makes it sound like a fairy tale and soon I cannot keep my eyes open. Before I sleep, I wonder who whispered Bones awake. Who knew I was scared here in the dark, in need of a friend and a story?

chapter 12

Today my aunt is waiting for me in the kitchen. I try to keep my back to her as I gather what I'll need for the day. It's the Wednesday that Mrs. Duncan goes to the city. Bones and I figure we have at least two hours of digging time in her yard.

My aunt is still waiting. Time is so short that I wish she would say what she wants. My father usually leaves the house by dawn, but he is going to work late today. I see him by the kitchen door. He peeks in, sees me with my aunt, and slowly creeps away down the hall. He is trying to go silently but he is cartoon funny because each step he takes makes huge creaks.

"Sammy?" my aunt finally says.

"Yes." I roll my eyes so far back in my head that I must look like a zombie.

"I just want to talk to you for a minute." I wonder why she always buttons her tight-collared blouses all the way up.

"Sure," I say. I keep busy because I figure it will make her talk faster.

"Could you come and sit down here with me?" she asks.

"I really want to sit down, but I'm in a hurry this morning," I answer.

I want to tell her that Mrs. Duncan only visits her mother every other week and if we don't grab this opportunity we'll have to wait another two weeks.

"Please," she says softly.

I sit down across the table from her. I am close enough to see her eyelashes twitch. Her fingers pick at some invisible lint on her dress.

I start to sway and wave my legs up and down. I am annoying her.

"I'm going to be leaving soon," she says.

"Leaving? But you just got here."

"My work is almost done."

"Oh," I say, getting up.

"If you needed me to stay . . ."

"No," I say.

I lie all the time now. I can do it staring right into someone's eyes, though I don't stare into her eyes. I look at my powder white legs and the socks that are slipping down into my sneakers.

Bones knocks on the back door and I jump to

answer it. I pull her inside, stand behind her, and push her at my aunt like a shield.

"Good morning, Ms. Goodwin," Bones says. She turns to me. "Are you ready?"

"Just a minute," I say. "I forgot something." I fly out of the kitchen, down the hallway, and up the stairs to my room.

"Sammy, you okay? Got everything?" Bones follows me up the steps.

"I forgot my flashlight."

"Well, come on. Mrs. Duncan's already left. We only have until noon at most."

Bones goes downstairs and I hear my father talking to her. I look around on my floor, under my bed, and in the closet. Out of the corner of my eye I see a thin figure in blue standing by my bureau, but it isn't Bones or my aunt. I blink and when I look up, whoever was there is gone. I go to the door and look up and down the hallway.

"Sammy, what's the matter? Come on!" Bones is at the bottom of the steps with our two burlap bags over her shoulder.

"Did you just come up here again?" I ask.

"Nope, I was down here with your father. Why?" She's impatient. I run down the stairs and pull her out the door.

To get into Mrs. Duncan's yard, we dig away until we can shimmy under her fence and into her backyard. Since her property is entirely fenced in, no one can see us or know we're here. Bones doesn't even care if we get into trouble. She seems lost somewhere and when I ask her a question, she takes forever to answer.

"There it is, Sammy. Isn't it amazing?"

We are standing in front of the Lightning Rock. It is a hazy, humid day and little beads of water like tears trickle down the Rock. We settle in front of it, opposite a statue of the Virgin Mary. Half of Mary's flesh has fallen away from her face and the tiny pieces of paint lie in a circle at her feet. Her eyes are tired gray. She stands in her blue cloak with her arms outstretched, begging me to come closer. The tips of her fingers on her right hand are broken off. On the base of the statue are little foil holders like the kind expensive chocolates are wrapped in.

"Bones, it's a little creepy here," I say.

There is a path from the house to the statue. The rest of the yard is covered in stringy vines and dense patches of grass. Bones begins to tug at the thick grass with her hands. The clumps pull away easily from the soil. I watch her dig, first with her hands, then with a small trowel she takes from her burlap sack. I can't remember the last time I really looked closely at her. She is letting her hair grow and it grazes the tops of her shoulders. As she digs, it falls into her brown eyes and with dirty fingers she pushes it behind her ears.

I turn from Bones when I feel that someone is looking over at us from the corner of the yard.

"What's the matter with you today, Sammy?"

I blink and look away. "Seeing things."

I pull out tools from the burlap sack and begin to work. I hope, for Bones's sake, we find some relic, some magical piece buried beneath this Rock. Bones works on one side, I work on the other. We find a woman's shoe, a broken piece of black-and-white ceramic tile, and a rusted wrench. Every once in a while I hear Bones exclaim, but mostly she's disappointed in our finds.

After an hour of digging we stop to rest. She sits eating peanut butter crackers. I hope we find something here for her. I imagine her leaning over a huge treasure chest so full of gems and diamonds that they pour out over the edges.

"She doesn't have anyone to take care of her yard," says Bones. "Don't you love it here? I wish this were all mine. It's so peaceful."

I look around. Thick bunches of flowers, their petals brown and partly eaten away, hang off slumping bushes. The tops of two haggard trees have become entangled in their search for the sparse sunlight. The Virgin Mary and the Lightning Rock seem to be rotting away into the soil.

"I don't see it, Bones. I wish I could see things the way you do."

Also, there is no sound in this garden. I have not seen crickets or birds or any form of life, except Bones and me. I know that it's my imagination, but everything seems to be closing in around us.

"You could talk about her—your mother," Bones says. "It's okay with me."

"Don't want to," I say. "I may never want to."

We don't speak anymore and she starts digging again. I push my hands into the cool dirt, exposing layers of color beneath the surface. As it crumbles through my fingers I wonder how many hands have touched it before me. Was it undisturbed until I came here?

"Maybe Mary knows secrets." Bones motions to the statue that is forever watching us, whatever direction we turn.

Bones hits a rock. I help her dig enough space around it so we can place our hands under it and yank it free. Under the rock is something else. Bones gets her flashlight and peeks in.

"It looks like a box," she says.

We both lean over and throw the soil into the air like dogs.

"I still can't get at it," Bones says.

I see Mrs. Duncan out of the corner of my eye and I push Bones down in back of the statue.

Bones angrily shakes my hand free. "What's the matter with you?"

"She's home," I whisper.

"What! It's not time."

Bones pokes her head up and looks around the statue toward Mrs. Duncan's house. "How can she possibly be home? It's not even close to the time that she's supposed to come home."

"Maybe she didn't go to see her mother today. Come on, Bones, we'll come back later," I say. "If we get caught—"

"But we're so close, Sammy. I don't want to let go when we're so close."

We manage to pile some clumps of dirt over the hole. From a few feet away it looks fine. It's only when you get up close that you realize there's now a moat around the Lightning Rock.

I throw all the tools into the bag and pull at Bones's arm. She continues to dig. I see Mrs. Duncan's head at the back door.

"Anyone out there?" she screams. "Here, kitty, kitty."

Bones crouches down next to me and we become very tiny and quiet. I close my eyes and believe with all my heart that Mrs. Duncan can't see us. I invent a dialogue with her in my head. In my thoughts, I am explaining why I am here in her yard, covered in her dirt, touching her things. It is going well; she is smiling at me and rubs my head. She says she feels sorry for me and she could help me along the way to salvation. She invites me in for tea and sweet biscuits. Her house is bright and smells sweet, like lilacs.

"I'm coming out there," Mrs. Duncan screams. "I've got a knife and I'm coming out there."

"Come on, Bones," I say, jumping up. I grab all our things and squeeze her down the hole and through to the other side. Her angry eyes could slice open my heart.

Once protected by the fence, Bones throws her burlap sack down so hard that it splits in half.

"Aargh!"

She stands for a moment, collects herself, sighs, picks up the tools, and puts them in my sack. She says nothing else to me. We walk to her house. I break the silence.

"You think she's been eating chocolates out there?" I ask.

"What do you mean?" Bones asks.

"There's those chocolate wrappers by the statue."

Bones thinks for a while.

"They're not chocolate wrappers, Sammy. They're from candles. Someone's been out there lighting candles."

She starts to smile.

"What?" I ask.

"You gave me an idea, Sammy," she says, sitting in front of her house. "Do you have any of those candy bars left that we got in the mail? Remember?"

We found this offer on the back of a cereal box that said if we ordered a hundred of this company's candy bars we were eligible to win a junior scientist kit. It contained a microscope with fifty slides of various dead things and a chemistry set we could use to make stink bombs. We always wanted our own laboratory.

The candy bars were delivered on the hottest day last summer. My mother and father stared at me as the mailman brought five boxes into our living room.

I think I almost had them convinced that everything was fine, until we sampled them. They tasted like moldy bread. I had never seen my father spit out food before.

We couldn't return the candy bars because the company didn't want them back. My father paid for all of them. And even though they were too horrible to eat, they were wrapped in beautiful silver paper. It seemed a sin to throw them out, so we put them in the basement. A few weeks later we did get the junior scientist kit in the mail. The microscope we had waited so long for arrived broken. There were only ten slides and five of them were of fly wings. The chemistry set consisted of one test tube and a coarse orange powder that Mr. Gold said was colored salt.

"Yeah, I got two boxes of chocolates in the basement."

"I think I have a plan to get us some more digging time," Bones says.

chapter 13

It is early in the morning, but I have been awake for hours. I turn the clue over in my hands. I hear the screen door close and I watch my father walk under the streetlight and into the darkness.

I look at the library book. I want to keep it longer and just stare at my mother's name. Later I'm going back to the library to see if she wrote her name in any other books. How many can I take out at one time?

I stare at the black-and-white picture my aunt gave me. I lay out Bones's diagram of the town. I count the streets from my house to Shadow Lake Park. I lay out the old map of the park, the one that fell from the library book. I read the clue again and again. My aunt knocks on my door and I push all my papers under a stack of clothes.

"Come in."

"Everything okay?" she asks.

"I just can't sleep sometimes," I say, turning to face her.

"I'm going down to make some tea," she says. "Do you want anything?"

"No, thanks."

"Oh, here." She places the repaired macaroni necklace around my neck.

As I hear her walking down the hallway, I twirl the macaronis on the string and return to my desk. I uncover my papers and get the familiar sense that there is someone at my door. I know when I turn no one will be there, so I just stare at the maps in front of me, ignoring the fact that whoever it is has come close enough to look over my shoulder.

Later, when I go to the library, the librarian sees me, opens her binder, crosses out "$2" and replaces it with "$1.75."

"You shouldn't have done that," I say. "I haven't finished reading it. Books like that are hard for me." I wait for her to erase what she's written.

"Come on, let's see what we can find for you," she says kindly. I follow closely behind her.

"How about this?" She stops, pulls a thick, brightly colored book from the shelf, and hands it to me.

I open the book and start to read the first page. She looks at me for my opinion.

"Too difficult?" she asks.

I nod my head, looking to see if she is disappointed in me. Perhaps she thinks I will be like Bones, who can easily glide through any book.

"It took me a long time to read well. No one in my family ever read anything. Then," she says, "I found something I truly loved." She bends her head toward mine.

I know she will say some English writer's name or worse, some French writer. I will have to look hopeless and just smile, knowing that I will never read those books.

"Comic books," she says.

"Really?"

"Oh, yes. I would read them in my room under the covers. I couldn't wait each month for the new ones to come out."

I try to imagine her hidden under the sheets late at night with her flashlight shining on the brightly colored pages. I can see in her eyes, just for a moment, someone there like me.

She chooses another book that is thinner, with shorter words. She also writes down the name of one of the comic books.

"I'm not sure they still publish it anymore." She puts her finger to her lips. "Our secret."

The librarian returns to her desk and I go through the shelves and pull out the oldest books. I turn to the inside back covers and search for my mother's name, but I have no luck.

On my way out, the librarian looks up from her desk and asks, "Is there anything else you needed?"

"Yes," I answer. "But I don't think it's here."

chapter **14**

"Try it one more time, Sammy. It doesn't sound very realistic," Bones says, shoving tools into her new sack.

"Mrs. Duncan, I was wondering if you would like to support the Sisters of the Congo and purchase one of these delicious chocolate bars."

Bones rolls her eyes.

"Come on, Sammy. If we get back to the yard, maybe we could even find Dr. Andrews's pocket watch." I have told her the story of Aunt Constance and Mrs. Duncan.

"I don't want to do this, Bones. Please," I say, getting down on my knees, "do not make me do this."

The candy bars from the basement are musty. They have lost their silver shine. I wonder if something has been at them, but I'm afraid to open them to look. If

Bones's plan works, Mrs. Duncan will not even be eating the chocolate. It's to distract her, so Bones can return to digging in the yard.

"Bones, I'm not brave enough."

"All you have to do is knock on Mrs. Duncan's door and try to sell her some dumb chocolate bars." I know she's frustrated with me. "Sometimes, Sammy, you just have to be brave."

"You know," I say, sitting down on the curb, "if she eats one, she may die and you'll have to carry that with you for the rest of your life. That you killed someone."

"She's not going to eat one. She's going to feel sorry for you because your mother died. She's going to think you need direction and guidance," Bones says, but I know she wants to take it back immediately.

She sits down and pulls her long legs up to her chin. "I just mean—Oh, Sammy, please just do it. Please just do it, as hard as it is, 'cause I got a feeling there's really something there."

I can't say no to her. The day my mother was buried, I wouldn't leave the cemetery. I told Bones I couldn't leave my mother there alone because it's scary to be left all alone in an unfamiliar place. Bones stayed with me and we kept my mother company until the stars came out.

I watch Bones take the bandanna from around her neck and wipe her forehead. I mess my hair up and write my name with a stick in the gravel at my feet.

"Okay, but just once. If it's not enough time, I'm not doing it again," I say.

"All I need is a few minutes to finish digging it out. Promise."

"Bones?" Part of me wants to tell her about the buried jewelry box and the clue, but part of me wants to solve the puzzle myself. "Never mind, I can tell you later."

We start our walk to Mrs. Duncan's house. I tried to make the candy bars look attractive. I got out some old red ribbon and tied it around two of the bars, the most I thought she'd buy. I'm wearing a Sunday white shirt that's too large around the collar, but Bones says it makes me look small and pathetic. At the corner before the house, Bones leaves me.

"Just a few minutes is all I need. Okay?" She gently shakes my shoulder. "Okay?"

"Yes," I say finally.

Bones runs around the corner. She will be in place soon. I walk slowly and try to imagine that there really is a Sisters of the Congo. Without me they would die because they're living off of red bugs and malaria water.

I quickly ring Mrs. Duncan's doorbell. I hear movements inside, but she does not come to the door. I ring again. The curtain flutters and she finally answers.

"Yes?" Mrs. Duncan says very softly, opening the door a crack.

"Mrs. Duncan?" Her face looks yellow and thin.

"Yes? Who's there?"

"It's Samantha."

"What can I do for you, Samantha?"

I'm going to tell her all about the Sisters of the Congo and the red bugs, until I forget my speech. As she opens the door wider I can see into her living room, where she must have been sleeping. The threadbare sofa is covered with well-worn, baby-soft quilts, and little bottles of medicine are stacked in towers on the floor beside it.

"Are you feeling okay?"

She is starting to shake herself awake. Her eyes are getting smaller and the muscles in her cheeks start to twitch. She doesn't seem that awfully glad to see me all of a sudden.

"Well, I just wanted to come check on you," I say. "They say to do that sometimes to older people in the summer, you know, just check on them."

She isn't saying anything to me. I am backing away and nodding at her, hoping Bones has gathered everything she needs.

"Wait just one minute. What's that you got there?" Mrs. Duncan asks in her cranky voice.

"Oh, nothing."

"Well, it just can't be a box of nothing, child," she says, pulling at it.

"I'm selling candy bars for the Sisters of the Congo."

"I'm not familiar with their work. What do they do?"

"Oh, they work very hard to bring the word of the Lord to people of the Congo. They're short nuns."

"Short?"

"Yes, to fit in with the Congonese."

"Well, how much are the candy bars?" she asks. I'm really afraid now that she will actually buy one and try to eat it.

"They're very expensive. They're two dollars each."

"To spread the word of the Lord, you say? Well, I think I can manage one. Hold on."

I tense my whole body as she turns away. I will never see my mother again because I'm going to be sent to a tiny, deep part of hell that no angel can ever enter.

She grabs her purse and digs down to the bottom and pulls out dimes and nickels, but it is not enough. She disappears and returns moments later with a ragged sock full of change.

"Mrs. Duncan, they're not very good," I say.

She continues counting out pennies. "They never are." She hands me the money and takes one of the ribboned bars.

"You know, Samantha, when I was younger, I lost people who were very important to me." I stand there holding the box of chocolates and wonder if she took some secret potion that turned her gentle. "Would you like a glass of milk or a piece of chocolate?" she says, starting to unwrap the bar.

I shake my head. "No, thank you. Well, I'm sure this will help the Sisters of the Congo." I turn away.

She closes the door and I walk, then run to the corner. I stop myself from screaming for Bones. I turn the corner searching for her, but she is nowhere to be seen. I walk in back to see if she is still coming out from under the fence.

"Bones?" I whisper.

"Sammy, I can't get it under the fence. Can you dig it out from there?"

She passes me the trowel. I dig quickly, pulling the dirt back with my hands until there is finally enough clearance to get the box through. Bones gives it one great push and I pull hard. I fall back, with it lying against my chest. Bones crawls through, then quickly shovels dirt back into the hole.

"Open it!" I say.

"No, let's take it somewhere safe first."

"How can you be so patient?" I ask, following at her heels.

"Is anyone home at your house?" she asks.

"Let's go there. We'll just take it in the backyard."

We try to cover up the box the best we can, though it still peeks out from the bag. It smells like earth and dampness. Part of the bottom is soft and weak. I am afraid it will crumble on the way home and all our treasures will trickle out onto the pavement. The walk to my house seems torturously slow. When we turn my corner I can see my father outside talking to Dr. Andrews. I pull Bones around and we cut through the backyards of the houses until we reach mine. I peek in the windows to see if my aunt is in the kitchen. She's not.

We lay the box down in the backyard and stare at each other.

"What's the matter?" I ask.

"Something doesn't feel right. Let's just open it and get it over with."

She sticks the tip of the trowel into the little crack that separates the top from the bottom. She shifts her weight and I watch as the rotted wood easily gives way. There is one nail we can't get out, but we are able to slide the top out and away from the bottom. I want Bones to look first because she deserves it. She leans over the wooden box and then looks up at me. She seems to melt and I think instantly of all the curses connected to ancient things.

"What's the matter?"

Bones sits on her knees and slowly puts her hands to her head.

"What's the matter? What's the matter?" I scream.

"Oh, Sammy, what have we done?"

I look down in the box and it only takes me a few seconds to understand. The figure is so tiny. Its head is turned slightly away from me and mostly covered by a frayed white bonnet. Someone dressed her in a pink sweater and buttoned it, to keep her warm.

There is a tiny blanket at the bottom of the box. We must have jostled it from her with our clumsy movements and careless footing.

"It's someone's baby," Bones whispers as she covers her eyes with her hands.

I stand over the box confused. "Is this our treasure, Bones?"

"Don't keep looking at it!" Bones says. She grabs at me to pull me away and my foot gently knocks the box.

I look down and notice that a tiny plump arm is exposed. On the hand two of her fingertips are cracked, others broken. I reach in and gently touch her.

"What are you doing!" Bones screams.

"Look," I tell Bones, pulling her close. I can see the doll's face now. There are tiny, thin lines running through the white porcelain, a touch of pink still in her cheeks. Her gray-blue eyes stare up at us, making her seem eerily alive. Though someone tucked her in years ago, she has never slept.

"A doll?" Bones whispers.

"Whose is this?" I say, turning to her.

"But where's our treasure?" says Bones. As I watch her, she slowly starts to come apart. She hits her fist on the ground. "It's not ever what it's supposed to be! This isn't for us." She frantically tries to slide the lid back into place. "Nails. We need some nails."

"We can't put it back like this. We opened it. We dug it up." My stomach aches. There's blood in my mouth from where I've chewed the skin off my bottom lip.

"I'll take it back and bury it tonight," Bones says. My father walks into the backyard. He comes over to us and we slowly back away from the box.

"What in God's name?" he says, staring down at the doll.

I can hear Mrs. Duncan down the street. She is already screaming. I know she is coming to get what is hers. She runs into my backyard, waving a large stick.

"You horrible girls. Are you happy now?" she screeches. She heads right for us. My father pushes me and Bones behind his back.

"You're nothing but savages." She is so angry that foam is forming on her lips. I think she is going to throw the stick at my father, but instead she stabs it into the ground by our feet.

Aunt Constance runs from the kitchen into the backyard.

"You put them up to this, didn't you?" Mrs. Duncan says, inches from Aunt Constance's face. "After all these years—"

"No," I say. "She didn't know anything about it."

"This"—Mrs. Duncan points to the box—"is mine. It's all I have left."

"It's just a doll," I say softly.

"You!" she says, coming closer to both Bones and me. "You will never understand how precious . . ."

Her eyes are filling with tears and she is unable to speak. Aunt Constance goes to her, but Mrs. Duncan pushes her away.

"I'm sorry," I whisper as Mrs. Duncan falls to her knees by the box.

She carefully rearranges the small blanket, tucking it gently around the doll. She whispers a short prayer, waits a few seconds, then slides the cover closed.

I feel my father's arm grip my shoulder. "We thought it was something magical," I mumble through my tears. "All we wanted was something magical."

chapter 15

ᏚᏓᎦ

I sit in the hallway outside the kitchen. No one will speak to me. Bones has left. Her mother pulled her by the arm all the way home.

I am supposed to be in my room. Against her will, Mrs. Duncan is sitting in my kitchen with Aunt Constance. My father and Dr. Andrews are talking by the back door.

Though Dr. Andrews doesn't practice medicine anymore, he brings his black bag and sits with Mrs. Duncan at the table. He takes her hands in his. I crane my neck to watch. He takes out an old stethoscope and he listens for her heart.

"Try to calm down, old girl," he finally says, and pats her arm. "Now, what's this nonsense I hear you talking?" he says gently.

I close my eyes because I think it will help me to listen.

"You can tell everyone," Mrs. Duncan says. "I guess most everyone knows already."

Dr. Andrews sits back in his seat. "Most everyone knows what?"

"That it was all my fault," she says. "What happened to Annie."

"Your sister's death?" asks Dr. Andrews, very surprised.

I open my eyes wide. Mrs. Duncan doesn't say anything; she just nods.

"Aurora," he says, leaning close to her. "No one is to blame for such a horrible thing."

"But I survived," says Mrs. Duncan. "I was the first one to get scarlet fever and I infected her. I should have died. She was so young, only five."

Dr. Andrew sighs. "But, Aurora, the fever weakened her heart. There was nothing that could be done for her. We didn't have the medicines back then. It's not your fault."

"She was my only sister," says Mrs. Duncan. "They were taking all her toys away and I didn't want her to be left with nothing. I took the doll, scrubbed it the best I could. I dressed it, saved it." She lowers her head. "I had waited so long for a sister."

"I know," Dr. Andrews says, patting her hand. "I know. You were a good sister too, Aurora."

They sit for a minute around the table. Finally Mrs. Duncan gets up and goes through the back door. Dr. Andrews follows her. Aunt Constance stands in the doorway, blocking my view. I scurry out the front door and run around to the backyard.

Mrs. Duncan goes to the box and pushes the cover back. She reaches inside and pulls out a tiny satin bag that must have been hidden in the blanket. She offers it to the doctor. He hesitates.

"Please," Mrs. Duncan says. "Take it."

She gently drops the bag into his open hands. He removes the contents and holds it up to the fading light. The pocket watch swings back and forth, glimmering.

"I'm so sorry," Mrs. Duncan says. "I just wanted her to have something special."

The doctor hangs his head. My father comes out and wraps the box in a clean sheet, strapping it onto the red wagon. He looks at me, but I hide behind the bumpy metal garbage can, breathing like I've run for miles. When I hear steps close to me I bolt for the front door.

I look out the window of my dark room and watch as Aunt Constance walks Mrs. Duncan home. Mrs. Duncan pulls the red wagon. The one broken wheel spins and squeaks. On the way down the street, porch lights come on and I watch my aunt and Mrs. Duncan wander in and out of the pools of light, finally disappearing into the darkness.

"I'm so sorry, Mrs. Duncan," I whisper.

I go to wash my face, and through the small window in the bathroom, I hear my father and Dr.

Andrews talking in the backyard. I turn off the light and stand on the hamper so I can watch. Soon the doctor walks away, leaving my father alone.

I watch him until I am almost asleep at the window. Finally I go to bed. I lie there forever thinking. When I turn to look at my door I see my father standing there, but he doesn't come in.

"How long have you been there?" I ask.

"A while."

"I really am sorry about everything," I say.

"I know," he says. "You okay?"

I shrug. Can he see that in the darkness? He comes toward me and sits on the corner end of my bed.

"Have I ever had scarlet fever?" I ask.

"No, but even if you did, it's not like the old days. It's very sad because only a year or so later they had medicines that probably could have saved her sister Annie."

"How come Mrs. Duncan didn't die?"

I listen to my father shuffle his feet back and forth. "Well, her sister's illness developed into a fever that affected her heart."

"And that was her sister's doll?"

"The disease could spread so easily that they used to burn all the children's belongings. Mrs. Duncan saved the most precious thing her sister had and buried it."

"We're not going to get sick, are we, 'cause we opened the box?"

"No, it can't hurt you anymore."

"She buried it at the Lightning Rock," I tell him

softly. "Maybe she was hoping that its magic would save her sister."

"Sometimes not even the greatest magic—" My father stops and we sit silently.

"She lights candles for her sister. I saw them."

"I didn't know that," my father says.

I turn over to face him. "What happens to your heart when you die?"

"There's nothing to feed it, so little by little it fades away," he tells me.

I think of Mrs. Duncan reburying the box and how each day she will visit it. My mother is buried in a cemetery that I rarely go to. I think of the tiny limbs of the doll wrapped in its sweater and warm blanket. I think of my mother, buried in only a blue dress. I should have thought to send something with her, like Bones says the Egyptians did when they buried their queens: pieces of gold, elegant necklaces, a pocket watch.

"Good night," my father says.

"You could stay," I say.

He leaves, but moments later I hear furniture being moved. To get the chair into my room he has to turn it sideways. Then he clears a path to me by kicking the sweaters, puzzle pieces, and magazines out of his way. He puts his chair down by the tiny light at the head of my bed. He sits and reads the newspaper. He says nothing more to me. I watch his shadow on the wall, huge and protective. I think of tiny candles burning in ancient yards.

chapter 16

The whole neighborhood is talking about me and Bones. They whisper about us on their front porches and nightly walks and tell us to stay far away from their yards. They feel so sorry for Mrs. Duncan.

We are forbidden ever to dig again. Bones says she's tired of it anyway. Lately she studies the night sky and says she would rather look up to the stars than down to the ground. She tells me all the myths of the Greeks and Romans and she points out the constellations. I can never see them. We are spending less and less time together.

I thought once that nothing could ever stop Bones from digging, but she says she has dark dreams of bones and tiny hearts and things that are hopelessly lost. She says she knows it's all true now, about the Lightning Rocks. People did bury their precious things there, but no magic came of it. I think she has stopped believing.

Bones's mother pulled me aside one afternoon and said, "Bones is miserable, Sammy. Do you think she'll like this?" I expect it to be another dress, but instead it's a glossy science book.

When I walk to the library, I stop at Bones's house and call up to her bedroom window.

"I'm going to see Mr. Gold. Want to come?"

It takes her a minute to come to the window. "Nah, not today," she says, and lingers for a minute. I stand kicking a little at the grass; then I finally look up to the window and wave goodbye. When I reach Mrs. Duncan's house, I always cross the street to avoid it. Bones and I have written notes to her to say how sorry we are. We said we would take care of her back-yard—fill in the holes, plant flowers, mow the lawn. There was no response. I think of the peeling paint on the Virgin Mary statue and the well-traveled path from the house to the grave.

At the library, I push open the ancient door to see if Mr. Gold is inside his office.

"Hello, Sammy," he says in his hoarse voice. His eyeglasses are broken. What is left of them is fastened to his head with a piece of tape. "Come on around and have a look at this with me."

It is the most ancient of the maps. I smile when I see it unrolled on his desk.

"Careful, now," he says. "Watch the corners."

He drags over a rickety chair for me to sit in and together we look over the map like old explorers.

"Where is our friend Bones?" Mr. Gold asks.

I sigh. "Well, you know we can't go digging anymore. . . ."

"Yes, I had heard something about that," he says. "I stopped by to see Mrs. Duncan recently."

I look up at him, shocked.

"We're old friends," he says.

"You're friends with her?"

"Well, it is true that you have to look deep to find her true self. But you should know that treasures are never found on the surface."

"Did she mention me and Bones?" I ask, chewing on my bottom lip.

"Well . . . ," he says, taking a deep breath. "I do believe she referred to you once or twice."

"We said we'd fix everything. We said we would put the box back, right where we found it," I blurt out.

"That's not what she wants anymore. She's wiped the dirt away from the doll and keeps it on her mantel now, next to the pictures of her family."

"But doesn't it make her sad? Doesn't it remind her of her sister's death?"

"Actually," he says, clearing his throat, "I think it reminds her of her sister's life. She told me many wonderful stories of the things they did when they were young."

"Why did she let it lie there alone so long? Why didn't she dig it up?"

"It reminded her of many painful things too." He lifts his head and seems to focus on something in the distance. "It takes a brave soul to face the past, Sammy."

I look down at Mr. Gold's ancient map. I trace the swirling path to Shadow Lake Park.

"Oh, Sammy, I forgot to tell you!" Mr. Gold jumps out of his chair.

"What?" I ask, startled.

"Go to that big room downstairs."

He has been in the library since it was built, but he can never remember names. He always refers to people as "that woman in reference" and places as "that room with the maps" or "that big room where people meet."

"What's there?" I ask.

"Just go see," he says, readjusting his glasses. "Hurry."

chapter 17

I find the room on the bottom floor of the library. Inside are two gray-haired ladies arguing over something in one of the corner display cases. I start to investigate.

"Excuse me. The children's room is up one flight and over to the right," the taller one says. She turns back and starts chattering again to her friend.

"But I don't want the children's room. I was told to come here," I say, peeking into the cases.

"By whom?" the tall one asks. Both slowly walk toward me.

"Mr. Gold."

"You've seen Mr. Gold?"

"Sure, all the time."

"We've never had the honor of meeting Mr. Gold," the tall one says, folding her arms and sighing. "I hear he sits up there all day and drinks champagne and eats baby corn on the cobs."

"Oh, Mildred, he does not," the other lady says. Her speech passes her lips slowly. It is hard for me to wait as she takes breathy pauses after each word. Kind of like the way I read. "She's prone to exaggeration, you know," she says to me.

"What have you come to see?" Mildred asks.

"Well, I don't know," I answer.

"I told you these children today are slow, Julia."

"I'm not slow," I say, though I can't do much to prove her wrong.

"Well, there's nothing of interest here for you. This"—Mildred waves her hand—"is an exhibit about the Shadows. You wouldn't know what that was, dear."

"Yes, I do." I look into one of the cases.

There are snapshots and postcards, old ticket stubs, pictures of pie-eating contests and frog-jumping tournaments. "Oh, look at this," I say, laughing. There are beauty queens and strong men. Pictures of years and years of opening days.

"My dad used to work there when he was a kid," I tell them. I want to add that my mother worked there also, but I can't. The two women come a tiny bit closer to me.

"Mr. Gold sent you?" asks Mildred, and she squints so hard that I think her glasses will go all the way up her forehead.

"Yes, ma'am."

They eye each other and share some sort of secret code. I shuffle my feet and think I should just go get Mr. Gold.

"Just you?" says Mildred. I nod.

She waves me toward the cases. I'm sure they want me to be done quickly, but each item forces me deeper and deeper into the Shadows until I feel I am standing at the entrance begging to go in. Julia comes and looks over my shoulder. I think she is afraid I will not understand her because of her slow speech.

"On Sundays, my mother and father would row me around the lake. Once, on my birthday, we stayed late and I remember seeing the rides at night. The lights were reflected in the water. It was dazzling."

"My friend's mother says that the mist looked like angels dancing," I say.

"Sometimes it did," Julia says with a sigh.

Mildred tells me stories of her brother, who was the strong man for four summers. "Come here," she says, taking my hand and pulling me to the back display case. "There he is." The picture shows a tall man with a bright white smile holding barbells high over his head. "They used to have weight competitions every Saturday where all the boys would come and test their strength. My brother was undefeated." She opens the display case and turns the picture slightly as if to make him more comfortable.

"Oh, Julia, what fun we had! Didn't we, dear?"

I move from case to case. Looking down, I stand

before the infamous Pegasus. I shudder. It is sitting in a beautiful flowered field looking truly majestic and frighteningly alive.

"Oh, I hated that horrible, haunted thing," Julia says, leaning over my shoulder.

"That's because you were afraid of it," Mildred says.

"Oh, hush, you. I swear it was alive. Everyone knew it too. I can still see its bright white wooden slats and hear the clatter of the cars."

There are pictures of Pegasus alight against the night sky. "It's beautiful," I say.

"It really was something. We'll never seen anything like that again," says Mildred. I look carefully through the two dozen pictures they have of the roller coaster.

"What are you looking for?" Julia softly asks me.

"My father worked at Pegasus in the summers. I was hoping there was a picture of him here." Actually I was hoping there was a picture of my mother. Mildred shows me the few photos that were saved in a box underneath one case.

"These just weren't that interesting," she says, handing them to me. "They came out of some old manual." They were boring black-and-white pictures of the roller coaster and the underground machine room.

I hand the pictures back to Mildred and look into the Pegasus case once more. I imagine myself in the first car at the top of the track. Any minute, gravity will capture me and force me forward. The fear of it makes me clench my teeth and hold tightly to the edge of the case.

Julia and Mildred are arguing in front of the pictures of ballroom dancing. Julia turns to me and starts telling me a story about her boyfriend, Richard, who was a dance instructor and had once danced with a Hollywood starlet.

"He had some unfortunate fake Spanish accent," Mildred says.

"You were just jealous because he was devoted to me," Julia argues.

The last case I look in is the one that interests me the most, the one about the Lightning Rock. There is a statue of it that Julia says used to light up, but it doesn't work anymore. There are pictures showing the mayor shaking hands with the governor in front of the rock. There are young women in wedding dresses and men in tuxedoes, leaning on it like it was another guest. There are children on May Day waving ribboned wands.

"They say it's buried so deep that the other end is sticking out in China," says Julia.

"Don't you ever wonder where it came from?" I ask.

"Well, talk about haunted," says Mildred.

"Don't be telling tales now, Mildred, and scaring the child."

"What?" I say.

"Well, one night a boy took a hammer and broke off a tiny piece of the rock. Supposedly it bled."

"We did not see this," adds Julia. "It's only hearsay."

"But our friends saw it," says Mildred. "And until this day they still talk about it. That boy ended up going crazy and was sent to a home down South for the rest of his life."

Julia rolls her eyes a little. "So many stories and so many memories came from that place. It was so powerful, the center of our world."

"Why did it close down if so many people loved it?"

"Well, we all grew up, didn't we?" says Julia softly.

"We always expected it to open again. I guess we're still waiting for it to come back to life," says Mildred.

Julia pulls her friend's arm. "Come on, I'll fix you a cup of coffee."

I watch them walk slowly out of the room and once they leave, I rummage through the box of unused pictures again. I borrow the ones of Pegasus. I promise myself that I will return them when I bring Bones in to see the display.

On my way out the door, I see a variety of group photographs taken at the gates to the Shadows. One shows ten or twelve young girls, maybe a year or two older than I am. They have their arms around each other and their legs raised as if they're dancing. I'm certain the middle two are Mildred and Julia. Their faces have changed so little. I think of Bones and me. I wonder if our journey together will last as long.

chapter 18

I am always the one in class who has the wrong answer. I remind myself of this as I lie in bed going over the clue in my mind, believing that I have solved it.

Go to the one that carries the Lightning

Well, that would be the Lightning Rock.

Go to the place that holds all the power

I think of what Mildred and Julia said about the power of the park.

Count seven steps

From the rock.

There I will be

That's where the jewelry box is buried.

I wait for you hour by hour.

It's waiting for me, just for me.

I think of calling Bones and explaining about the clue. She would know where to look, but I want very much to figure it out for myself. I want to be smart enough. I want something that is only mine. I stare at the black-and-white picture. It's all I think of. I have hidden it so many times, but I keep returning to it. I wish my aunt had never given it to me. I only want to see the other part of the picture, the face.

I lie in bed. I want to call Bones, and I wonder if maybe she is awake and staring up at the stars. I take one of the magazines from the stack we got from Ash. I turn on my light and read a story about a rose that blooms in winter in a garden in Angel Falls.

The next morning I'm waiting for the bus to Shadow Lake Park. I must take this bus, I keep telling myself. There is no other way.

I figure if I leave midmorning, it will be less crowded and there will be little chance of running into someone I know.

In my pocket, I have five dollars that I found in my mother's top drawer. My bag contains the clue, maps, a heavy flashlight, my trowel, and the pictures of the roller coaster I got from the library exhibit about the park. I have packed a snack and some water. I decide not to leave a note because I'll be back long before dark.

I go to a farther bus stop, not the one that is closest to my house. I wait with a tall man in a business suit who is reading a newspaper folded perfectly into long sections. He has a system for turning the pages over and inside out to continue reading the stories.

Many kids my age take the bus, though I never have alone. I sit on the bench, and though it's a cool day, sweat drips down my back. My heart speeds and I think of strange things like the color of the wallpaper in my room. Finally, when the bus comes, the door opens and I trip climbing up the few stairs.

"Watch your step there," the driver says to me.

I drop in my money and find two empty seats. I sit by the window with my backpack in the seat beside me.

I take a deep breath. This is the first time I've ever had to take notice of these streets. My mother always was the one to watch the stops and tell me when ours was next. Everything looks different when you're alone, like when the leaves fall from the trees and you suddenly see a house through the bare branches. People get on the bus and I try to remind myself that they don't always die when they try to get off.

Do I see different things than my mother did when she rode this bus? She always pointed out the colors of the fruit-and-flower stands. She would notice the brightness of someone's raincoat or the pictures that were painted on the side of the building. I only notice how far I am from where I started and how far I have to go.

The bus driver stops at the museum. I hear him say, "Careful now." I'd like to ask him if he was driving the bus the day my mother was killed. Would he remember her; could he forget her? Did she speak to him? Were her last words that she loved me? I think of my room at home, which holds most of what she ever owned, and still I can't get her back. There is everything of hers there, but there is nothing of her. I don't know where to look to find her anymore.

The bus is emptier now, so I move toward the front. The blocks are wider apart and have fewer flower stands and more liquor stores. There are dirty couches and mattresses lying on the sidewalk. Someone raises his fist and yells at the bus as it goes by.

I get out the street map that Bones made and look to see where I am and how much farther I have to go. I panic because, outside the bus window, I can't see the street signs clearly. Some are missing; others dangle and sway. Bones has written the names of the streets so small that I'm not sure if I'm reading them correctly. I'm probably miles from where I want to be.

The bus driver wears dark glasses and chews on a toothpick. The only other people on the bus are an elderly Asian couple. They speak in whispers. The bus passes sagging storefronts with blackened doors.

People gather at the street corners, sipping from drinks hidden in paper bags. My heart beats wildly. I think of how unprepared I am. The couple smiles at me.

"I'm a little lost," I tell them, but they don't hear.

I can't remember the voice of my mother. Though I close my eyes and concentrate, I can't hear the safe words she would have said.

It starts to rain. I can see nothing through the beads of water on the window.

"Where is it you're going?" the bus driver asks me.

I tell him.

"Not that many people go up that far anymore. You going on a science trip or something? You know that the last bus back is five-forty-five, right?"

"I'll be home way before then," I say.

"I hope so, because I wouldn't want to be there at night. That's when the bogeyman comes out of the mist and picks your bones clean."

chapter 19

"You sure this is where you want to be?" the bus driver asks as I get off the bus.

"Yes," I say. He keeps the door open for a minute in case I change my mind. Finally he closes it and pulls away.

I thought I would be at the entrance to the park, but I think I'm on the side of it. There is a tall, long fence with rolled barbed wire on top. I start to walk the length of the fence, hoping there's a hole I can squeeze through. I can't believe I'm here but can't get in.

I stop and take the map of the park out of my pack to see if I can get my bearings. I think I'm heading toward the lake that is at the very end of the park. The fence must stop before the water. I'll be able to get inside, but then I'll have to backtrack to the Lightning Rock, which is in the middle of the park. I'm wasting time. I'm nervous about being stuck in such a deserted place. Though I haven't seen any cars, I keep close to the fence and away from the street.

I walk for blocks, seeing no one and getting only occasional glimpses of the park through the trees. I think of Bones and the familiar streets of home.

By the time I finally see the lake my hair is matted with rain. The street that is running parallel to the fence ends in a circle for those who want to turn around. The fence extends a little into the lake, so I'll have to wade out into the water to get around it and into the park.

There is a multicolored car at the end of the road. It looks deserted. I go closer and closer, then walk past, glancing quickly inside.

There is a face in the window. Suddenly the door opens. I want to scream, but I'm afraid it will slow down my running.

"Hey! Are you here to steal my things?" the man in the car yells. He is trying to run toward me, but he trips over a rotted log.

I run into the water. I have to go in knee deep to get around the fence. He stops. He won't go into the lake. He watches me for a few minutes and then heads back to his car, screaming up to the sky.

I am soaked. My sneakers are full of tiny pebbles. I wipe dirt and tears from my face with the bottom of my shirt. I've made it to Shadow Lake Park.

Above the lake is a small pavilion where once you

could change into your bathing suit or wash the sand from your feet. The bathhouse is still there, but the doors and all the windows are missing. I walk in. Some of the floorboards are gone; others have huge holes in them. Hanging off a rusted nail on the wall is a tiny rag. As I get closer I realize it is a child's bathing suit that must have been forgotten many summers ago.

I turn and look at the lake. It's a dark day and hard to tell whether it's noon or dusk. My eyes start to play tricks on me as I watch small patches of mist form into figures that glide across the water's surface. They're beautiful to watch, but I turn my head away. I am afraid they'll lure me into the deep water.

I walk over a small hill that meets the path leading around the park. I see no one, though I feel like I'm being watched. I step under a tree and pull my map from my pocket. The path is winding. It would be faster for me to walk through the fields to get to the Lightning Rock.

The knee-high grass clings to my soggy pants. I wonder if these fields would still look as sad on a brighter day. Where I'm now walking, red-and-white tablecloths were held down by picnic baskets. Adults listened to music and danced; children played tag or catch. At night they all lay on their backs, side by side, and stared at the stars. So many things have been lost in this dirt.

In a clearing, I start to stumble over pieces of Kiddy

Land. The rides are gone, but there's a sign sticking up from the ground advertising Italian ices for ten cents. I try to pull the sign out, but it is buried deep and its edges are sharp and hard to hold.

It's so lonesome here. The park must be waiting for everyone to come back. It was so loved, then deserted.

I check my map. The Lightning Rock is over a small ridge that should be ahead of me and to my left.

I have to pass the garbage valley. I remember it from the tour Bones's uncle gave us. This valley is close to the road, and people throw their trash over the fence and into the park. I cover my nose with the neck of my shirt, but nothing can dull the stench of the hundreds of garbage bags that are broken open.

I hear rustling among the trash and a mangy dog lifts his head to sniff the air. I freeze. I expect he'll make a run for me but he seems much more interested in whatever he's found among the bags. When he returns to his feast, I back away slowly. Bones's uncle says sometimes people dump animals here when they become too difficult to take care of.

I want to rest, but I'm afraid to stop walking because I know I'll get scared. As I reach the tip of the ridge, I hear yelling. I run into the grove of trees to my right. I slowly move forward, shielded by the thick tree trunks. In the clearing over the ridge, three teenagers are sitting on a bench smoking cigarettes and laughing. I'm lost. The Lightning Rock should be close to them and Pegasus should be over the hill. I can't see either of them from here. In the distance I hear barking. The dog lifts his head, sniffs the air, and starts heading in my direction.

There's one good climbing tree. I manage to get two limbs up before I become dizzy. If the dog is a good jumper, he can easily reach my ankles. I hear Bones say, "Sometimes, Sammy, you just have to be brave." I get halfway up the tree and rest against a thick branch. The dog has picked up two friends. The three barking dogs circle the bottom of the tree. I look out to see the teenagers, but I almost lose my balance because past them, in the distance, rising from the earth, is Pegasus.

It is completely covered in many shades of green. Trees have grown through its wooden slats and vines have twisted around its rails, tying it tightly to the ground. Even now it is magnificent.

The teenagers, two girls and a boy, hear the barking and look around to see if the dogs are heading for them. They rise and start to walk away from the clearing. The dogs look around and run after the three teenagers. The girls and the boy throw rocks at the dogs but soon give up and run quickly toward the front of the park. The dogs follow. I climb down the tree and run to the clearing.

I have thought so much about the Lightning Rock and its power. I imagined it might be waiting for me, but now I know I've come too late. What I thought was a bench that the teenagers were sitting on is the rock. It has been chipped away from the base and pushed on its side. It's covered in fading spray paint, and large chunks are missing from it. Along one edge there are hundreds of tiny gashes. Maybe it bled to death.

I count the steps from the base, but there are large holes dug in the dirt everywhere around the rock. Whatever magical pieces were once buried here were long ago dug up. The holes are filled with old coffee cups, scraps of shoe leather, and soda bottles. I open my backpack and take out my trowel as if there is something left to find in this dirt. I get down on my hands and knees and dig hard into the earth. I cannot stay ahead of the thick drops of rain, and soon I am elbow deep in mud. I throw the trowel into the fields and push my hands into the hole, praying to find *something*. I feel an object slip between my fingers and I grab a handful of mud and bring it to the surface.

I wipe the object on my jeans. It is only another coin: Take a ride on Pegasus. "No!" I scream, and fling it far into the air.

I sit on the rock and look around at the deserted park. No one's coming back here to save it, to take care of it. She's not coming back to save me, to take care of me. She really has left me all alone. My tears mix with the rain; they drop from my cheeks and get carried by small rivers into the holes I've dug.

My bag falls open, and out spills my soggy sandwich and the envelope with the clue. I take it and crumble it in my hand.

"See, you always get the wrong answer," I whisper.

The pictures I took from the exhibit at the library swirl in the mud. I don't know why I brought them; they don't really even show the roller coaster. They show the room underneath the roller coaster. The machine room that my dad talked about. In one of them, a man in a blue uniform is standing in front of a flight of stairs. He has his arms out, pointing to the chain of the roller coaster and a small electrical box on the wall. He has a bright, wide smile. I am tired and lost as I count the stairs behind him. There are seven.

I grab the clue and try to smooth it out. I reread it, even though I know it by heart.

"Oh, God," I say, grabbing everything and throwing it in my bag. I look at the Lightning Rock and realize my mistake. I look into the distance and know where I have to go.

chapter 20

I thought Pegasus would be less frightening up close. I try only to think of it the way my mother saw it, when she loved it so much on those summer days. Closing my eyes for one moment, I am allowed to see it that way. There are girls in their summer dresses laughing, daring each other to ride again. And there is my mother waiting in line, handing the token to my father, who has been waiting to see her. She is so beautiful. He is so in love with her that he lowers his head and blushes. When I open my eyes, they are gone.

Bones was reading me a story late one night. In Greek mythology, after Pegasus returned to Mount Olympus, he became the keeper of the thunderbolts for Zeus. Pegasus carries the lightning.

Go to the one that carries the Lightning
Go to the place that holds all the power

Count seven steps
There I will be
I wait for you hour by hour.

I almost have it now. I know that I am close, but it is getting late. I am nearly out of time. I will never make the last bus. In the distance, I can see the teenagers heading back this way.

My father said the machine room was here somewhere under the roller coaster. I walk around underneath the huge structure, hoping that the dangling wooden pieces from the track won't fall on me. The machine room could be buried anywhere. Think, I tell myself, think this through. I look for the place where the chain would have come from the room and up to the roller coaster.

I find it and start to stomp furiously around on the ground until I hear a hollow metallic sound. I push grass and dirt away and find a large metal ring. I pull with all my might, but it doesn't budge. I wonder if they've put a padlock on it. I frantically wipe clear the whole surface of the door. I grab the ring and once more pull hard. Nothing. I search for a stick strong enough to use as a lever. Finding one, I wedge it in the small place under the door and lean all my weight on it. There is a tiny squeak.

The teenagers stop to light a cigarette.

I try to maneuver the stick in a little farther under the door, and I push again. It's starting to open. I leave the stick wedged and pull on the metal ring.

There's a thunderous crack. The door gives way and hits my cheekbone. Tiny drops of blood fall on the steps leading down.

I pull out my flashlight from the pack. I am thankful for its weight now. It's the only weapon I have. I count the steps down, but I know how many there are. Seven.

I shine my flashlight on shelves loaded with old rags and tools. I push them off to look behind them. There is nothing. Hidden in one of the corners are a few old folding chairs, extra chain, and torn raincoats.

My heart is beating so fast that I'm afraid it will burst. I shine the flashlight on the walls. Right by the last step, hanging upside down on the wall, is an old clock.

I wait for you hour by hour.

I kneel down and search the floor. There is nothing here except a stack of moldy towels. I am about to kick at them, but I stop. I peel away each layer until the last towel falls apart in my hand. There it is. A small pink jewelry box.

I sit holding it tightly. I am so afraid to open it, to see what's inside.

Then I hear them. I turn off the flashlight and back into one of the corners. I hope it's too dark for them to come down the steps.

I close my eyes. I hear voices. My father's voice is

hoarse. I know he has been calling me for hours. I can say nothing, but I step into their light.

My father comes down the steps, pulls me to him, and lifts me up into his arms. I cling to him as he brings me to the surface.

chapter 21

Dr. Andrews says I will be fine after a bath and a good meal. I have a deep purple cut on my cheek. It may scar, he says, but as I grow it will start to fade. Everything will heal.

I am sipping strong, sweet tea in my kitchen. Aunt Constance has been so contained, but I see her start to vibrate slightly as if a wire in her has come loose and something is about to short out. She pounds the saucepan on the counter and turns to me and yells.

"If you ever do anything like that again, I swear to God if those junkyard dogs don't get you, I will. Why would you go there alone?"

I whisper, "I'm sorry." She turns back to the stove and takes a deep breath.

"Imagine, in that park all by yourself. Whatever were you thinking? You could have been killed." Her voice is getting softer and softer until finally she's just mumbling to herself. My father has been at the front door, thanking Bones's uncle for his help. Bones's uncle is swearing about something.

My father says good night and closes the front door. He comes into the kitchen and sits down next to me.

"How did you know where I went?" I ask.

"Ash came over this afternoon and asked if you were here. He told Constance that he had been at the museum this morning and as he crossed the street he saw a girl who looked a lot like you staring out the window of the bus. Said it had been bothering him all day."

I had been too busy thinking of my mother. I hadn't noticed him.

"So Constance called Bones, and Bones got worried and ran over to see Mr. Gold. I come home from work and everyone's searching the neighborhood for you. Even Mrs. Duncan's screaming your name at the top of her lungs. If that wasn't enough to scare you home, I don't know what would."

I try to smile, but it hurts.

I look over to the counter by the sink and see a familiar book bound with black electrical tape.

"I'm sorry," says Aunt Constance, returning it to me. "I took it from your room. You've been reading it so much lately, I knew it would help me to know where you were."

"Did you see?" I say, turning to the back cover and finding my mother's name.

My father nods and touches the name lightly.

Bones is at the back door. I run to hug her tightly.

"Your face," she says slowly. Small pools of tears form in the bottoms of her eyes.

"I'm okay," I say. "I'm okay."

She sits with me at the table and I unload my pack to show her all the maps and tell her about the park. I try to smooth out the clue so she can read it.

"You figured that out about the power room all by yourself?" she asks. I nod. "You're amazing."

My father holds the clue in his hand after listening to the whole story. "It's strange to see her handwriting," he says softly.

"So let me see the treasure," Bones says. I pull her along to the living room and show her the box in the middle of the floor. "You're so brave, Sammy," she says.

"I'm not so brave, because now I don't want to look inside."

My father comes and sits in the chair. I thought once the box was taken home it would somehow transform and shine like gold. It smells damp, and parts of it are black with mold. I reach in back for the key to wind it up. I'm surprised to find it still works. I put my fingers on the clasp. It is rusty and hard to open. I look at my father, who is leaning close to me.

"Go ahead, now."

The ballerina looks like she just woke from a very long sleep, but she still dances. There is an envelope inside. It is moist and I'm careful not to rip it. I open it. I pull out the other half of the picture. No wonder my aunt was so startled when we first met. I look exactly like my mother at this age. At our age. There is a note under the picture. It is not very long.

I knew that it was only a matter of time before you found me.
Love you always.

I hand it to my aunt, who is standing in the hallway.

"This is for you," I tell her.

"I'm not so sure of that," she says.

There is nothing left in the box. There is nothing more I need.

Bones's mother comes to get her, though I know Bones doesn't want to leave me. My aunt goes up to bed and my father and I sit. I might let go of the box tomorrow. I might not.

I do not know how to talk about her. I have kept her safe for so long in the quiet, afraid to give any of her away.

"What was she like?" I ask my father. "What was she like when she was younger?"

chapter 22

My father and I have talked until dawn. I go to wash my face and stare at my swollen cheek in the mirror. My father doesn't say anything, but I know this is usually around the time he leaves for work.

"Can I come with you?" I ask him.

"You are going to bed."

"Please, just this once?"

He sighs. "After all you've been through?"

"Please!" I beg.

"Okay, I guess it's time. Come on, but"—he whispers—"don't tell your aunt."

I know that she will already know. She's like that.

He gets me a sweater and we leave the house in the coolness of the morning. We do not walk far. At the end of a long block is a beautiful house made of brick. He unlocks the door and waits for me to go in.

"The light switch is right on the wall there."

I reach for it and turn the hall light on. The house is empty.

"Come on," he says.

I follow him into the dim living room. I'm not sure what I'm supposed to see here. He usually paints the outside of houses, not the inside. He turns the lights on in the living room.

"Aah," I say, breathless. "You did this?"

"You like it? The guy who owns the house bought it for his mother. He says she used to love her gardens. But she's been sick and can't get out very much. He wanted something special for her."

The walls behind him are covered with long lilies and twisty roses. On one side he has painted a meadow with tiny white star-shaped flowers. The garden covers the walls of the room.

"I thought he was nuts at first, asking me to paint the garden right on the walls. Now he wants to do it throughout the whole house. It's not too hard, except the really small flowers are hard for me to paint. I get cramps in my hands."

I pick up the art book that is lying on the floor. The pages are slightly warped.

"Darned thing about that book. I went to the library one day and found it all mangled in the shelf. Someone had stuck it in upside down. Strange, huh?"

I nod. I know that if I turn to the back inside cover my mother's name will be there.

"So, the guy wants this finished soon," he says, motioning to the walls. "I got to put in more hours. I don't like to come after work, though. I like being home for you, just in case you need something."

I look at him in front of his masterpiece. "It's so beautiful." I touch the walls.

He smiles. "She would have liked it, wouldn't she, Sam? Your mother would have thought it was really something."

I nod. I realize that she would do what I'm doing. She would sit and stare, take it all in; she would find something of herself in it.

He stands back to admire his work. He reaches his hand out to me. "Come on, Sammy. Time to go."

We walk out into the morning.

At home, he tucks me into my bed and lays the pink box on my bureau. I sleep until dinner. When I wake I look around my room at all the things I've collected of my mother's. I pick up a brooch with sparkly glass and I smile when I remember my mother pretending it was made of diamonds. Before I go to eat dinner, I return it to her room.

chapter 23

𝒾 am sitting on the front steps with Ash. My father is asking him about planting some trees and flowers in our yard. Ash is sticking his hands into our dirt and looking at the sun.

"Roses would grow great here," Ash says. "You'd need someone to weed and water and take care of things."

That means me, so I pretend I don't hear. "Sammy, go ask your aunt to come down. Let's get her advice," my father says.

I go upstairs and knock on her door. She invites me into her room. I look at the three boxes piled up against the wall. The ones we moved that first day.

"What's in all these?" I ask.

"You can look," she says. She is folding her blouses and putting them into a suitcase.

I open the boxes. They are filled with other people's pictures and letters and trinkets.

"How long do you keep this stuff for?" I ask.

"Somehow I can't throw it out," she says. "I guess it's what I collect."

"We could move it downstairs," I say, "to the basement with the chocolate bars."

"I'm not going to be here much longer, Sammy. I don't like to stay in one place too long. It's better to move around."

"Why?"

"So people don't find me."

"What happens if they find you?"

She looks at me but doesn't answer. I go and sit on the corner of her bed.

"You and your father don't need me," she whispers.

"I want you to stay," I say.

She stops packing and looks into my eyes. It makes me nervous having all her attention. I point out the window to my dad and Ash.

"They're making a garden. Come and see." I drag her out into the sunlight. She sits on the stair with me and looks over the flower catalogs. It's a wonderfully warm day, and my aunt undoes the top two buttons of her collar. My father and Ash stop talking. They are staring at something in the distance.

"Well, well, well," my father says. We're not the only ones to notice. I see my neighbors's heads bent together; they're whispering.

"What is it?" I say, getting up, but Bones is already at my gate.

She is laughing. "I'm surprised people aren't falling out of their windows." She's wearing a bright yellow dress. One of the hundreds her mother has bought for her over the years. "It's for my grampa's party." She shrugs.

I elbow her.

"My mom, she just tries so hard. We made a deal. If I wear this to the party she'll buy me this set of astronomy books from the secondhand store."

I touch the bottom of the dress. It feels soft. "It looks great," I say.

"You know, Mr. Gold has a telescope," says Bones.

"He does?"

"Says we can come over anytime."

She stares at me and pulls at my front bangs. "They grew back."

I lower my head and let them fall in my eyes.

"I got a list of houses I'm supposed to walk in front of, friends of my mother's." Bones laughs. She whispers something to Ash.

"No, I haven't told her yet," says Ash.

"What?" I ask.

"I have a friend who does some work for the parks department. He can hire fifty kids to do some cleanup across town," says Ash.

"At the Shadows," Bones blurts out. "My mom said I could do it. Do you want to?"

"I can probably get you in. I mean, if it's okay with your father," says Ash. My father doesn't say anything.

"I thought you were done with digging." I say to Bones.

"Maybe there's something out there for me," she says softly.

I think of Pegasus on the hill just waiting for companionship. Bones will get along just fine with it. It's her turn to find some treasures there.

"I was going to work on my dad's project," I say. My father turns to me, surprised. "Remember, you said your hands get tired. I could help paint."

"Well, even if you don't decide to help at the park, I can take you to have lunch with Bones," my aunt says. "I mean, if it's okay for me to stay around for a while."

"We'd like you to stay, wouldn't we, Sammy?" says my dad, nudging me.

"Yes," I say, smiling.

"I was thinking maybe I'd stay put for a while too, you know, do some more work on the house," Ash says, clearing his throat and looking at Constance. She turns away so Ash doesn't see her blush. Bones looks at me and rolls her eyes.

"I've got to go," says Bones, taking out her list of addresses. "Want to come?"

I touch my swollen cheek. "You go," I tell her. "But come back soon."

"Don't I always?"

As Bones walks down the street, Mrs. Duncan passes her. Mrs. Duncan stops for a minute to speak with her and then moves on toward my house. I get up to go hide inside.

"You stay right there, young lady," says my father.

Mrs. Duncan peers over the fence and stares into the dirt and dead grass. "Nice garden," she says to my father.

I have not seen her since the day she came into my backyard. I can barely look at her. "You okay?" she asks gently. I nod. "Did you find your magic, Sammy?"

"Yes. Want to see?"

Before she answers, I run inside and grab the picture of my mother. I have taped both halves together. I bring it out front and offer it to Mrs. Duncan. She takes it gingerly.

"Don't hide this away," she says softly, handing the picture back to me. "Put it where everyone can see it, Sammy." She holds my hand for a long moment before she continues down the street.

"Oh, about that chocolate," she says, turning back. "Worst stuff I ever had in my life. Terrible."

My aunt is talking to Ash and showing him pictures of purple and yellow flowers, while Ash shakes his head and points to the sun. My father sits next to me.

Though I don't fit very well anymore, I sit in my father's lap. He wraps his arms around me. I lie back and listen to his heart. He's holding something tightly in his hand. I pry his fingers loose and stare at the coin for Pegasus. He has cleaned it until it sparkles like a diamond.

Out of the corner of my eye, I catch a glimpse of blue. She is here with me. I hold her picture tightly and feel her draw a heart in the palm of my hand.

ABOUT THE AUTHOR

Adrienne Ross was born in New York and has lived on both coasts. One of her favorite hobbies is digging in the dirt with her kids, looking for something amazing. She lives with her husband and their three children in a western suburb of Boston. *In the Quiet* is her first published novel.